"I thought I told you to stay put!"

Jack's voice was a low growl, much like the harmless chuffing noises from the preserve's felines.

Emerson stiffened, an instinctive response to the constable's tone. "I don't do well with orders, Constable." Her lips curled into what she hoped conveyed her displeasure. Well-versed with how the law worked—and not always in her favor— Emerson was treading on unstable ground by potentially hindering police matters.

Constable Jack's Adam's apple bobbed. Whether from irritation or some other emotion, she could only surmise.

"It's my job to keep you safe!" His words tumbled out.

But then Jack reined in his thoughts right before her eyes. "To keep the preserve safe."

With sudden self-consciousness, she extricated herself from his solid strength. At the same time, she sensed his reticence to end their standoff as his arms fell to his sides.

Closing her eyes for a moment, she repeated her mantra. *It's not my job to fix him.* She also did not need him to assume the role of hero.

A self-professed princess, **Chris Maday Schmidt** believes it's always the "write" time for real-life fairy tales brimming with hope for new beginnings, humor in the messy middle and heart for happy endings. Originally from the Midwest, she relocated to the Southwest with her husband and daughter. She currently resides in Northern Arizona's Rim Country and writes wholesome stories about family, friendship and faith. Chris loves Jesus, reading, yoga and hiking. Visit chrismadayschmidt.com.

Books by Chris Maday Schmidt

Love Inspired

A Father's Vow

Visit the Author Profile page at LoveInspired.com.

A Father's Vow

CHRIS MADAY SCHMIDT

LOVE INSPIRED
INSPIRATIONAL ROMANCE

LOVE INSPIRED®

INSPIRATIONAL ROMANCE

Recycling programs for this product may not exist in your area.

ISBN-13: 978-1-335-59875-2

A Father's Vow

Copyright © 2024 by Christine T.M. Schmidt

All rights reserved. No part of this book may be used or reproduced in any manner whatsoever without written permission except in the case of brief quotations embodied in critical articles and reviews.

This is a work of fiction. Names, characters, places and incidents are either the product of the author's imagination or are used fictitiously. Any resemblance to actual persons, living or dead, businesses, companies, events or locales is entirely coincidental.

For questions and comments about the quality of this book, please contact us at CustomerService@Harlequin.com.

® is a trademark of Harlequin Enterprises ULC.

Love Inspired
22 Adelaide St. West, 41st Floor
Toronto, Ontario M5H 4E3, Canada
www.LoveInspired.com

Printed in U.S.A.

I will say of the Lord, He is my refuge
and my fortress: my God; in him will I trust.
—*Psalms* 91:2

My sincerest thanks
first go to my editor, Shana Asaro,
and assistant editor, Besarta Sinanovic,
for their confidence in my story
and for making my dream to write for
Harlequin Love Inspired come true.

Second, I couldn't have made it this far
without fellow writers TR, SA, LS and MB,
for giving me wings to fly.

Also, shout-outs go to Joel Harris, a retired fire
captain who was kind enough to answer questions
for this story (all errors are mine); to Mike Garcia,
whose perfectly sweet corn bread recipe is
mentioned in this book (modifications are mine);
and to the original Big Country—
you know who you are.

To my daughter, Bailey Ann, sisters, Diane,
Jan and Karen, and BFF Jennie, a heartfelt
thank-you for being my biggest cheerleaders.

Last, but not least, there will never be enough
words to express my love and appreciation
to my husband, Bob, my real-life hero.

Chapter One

You were born to serve and protect.

His late wife's words echoed in his ears. Never mind that he'd failed to live up to his oath in the worst way.

Now, all senses on high alert, Constable Jack Wells maneuvered his station-issued cruiser over the rutted gravel drive. The tires settled into the well-worn grooves as he made slow progress toward the wooded wildlife preserve and sanctuary. With his headlights off, he used extra caution to avoid potential contact with critters that may have escaped from the fenced-in property.

Peering into the shadows cast by the towering ponderosa pines, piñon pines and Douglas firs, their needles glinting in the light reflected off the stars twinkling in the night sky, Jack scanned the familiar surroundings. After opening the window, he leaned his head into the crisp autumn air, straining his ears. To hear what, he couldn't be sure. But because of the rash of targeted vandalism on the preserve at the edge of small-town Sweetwater—located in a mile-high basin in Northern Arizona—patrolling the grounds had become a routine event. Which, due to the station's staff shortage, often meant conducting his rounds off-duty.

And his job as the constable was to serve and protect.

That phrase again. A twig snapped in the distance, distracting his mind from traveling down a different kind of well-worn trail.

"Come out, come out, wherever you are," he whispered under his breath, the melody reminiscent of his life before loss.

He cocked his head, searching for sounds that were out of the ordinary. But he only heard the usual animals—an owl's hoot, unnerving giggles from a resident hyena and a few yips from a coyote. Most of the rescues slumbered now, safe within the confines of Sweetwater Preserve & Sanctuary and in the hands of its caring staff.

Continuing along the road, he peered into the shadows of the property run by the nonprofit. Not only was the preserve barely able to remain afloat, but it appeared to be wearing a big red target.

Nothing earth-shattering at this point—just petty occurrences on the grounds. But the probability that the culprits could step it up a notch by endangering the animals was not a stretch of the imagination.

And that was one thing he vowed would not happen. Even if the reasons he harbored were of a personal nature, rather than a professional one.

"Don't go there," he chided, voice low.

Advancing inch by inch along the gravel drive that funneled into the parking area situated in front of the preserve's main building, his left hand absently touched the sharp metal points on his badge. He shifted his hand, then, to the contrasting smoothness of the ring pinned next to it. His daily reminder of the one person he'd promised to protect when she agreed to be his wife. The one person he'd failed.

His best friend's voice—the words he'd spoken to him at Willow's memorial service three years earlier—sounded in his memory: *The Lord chooses where or not to heal on this side of heaven, but He's still our refuge.*

His throat constricted, the lump refusing to budge. His friend was right. Yet that knowledge would not bring back his child's mother.

Just then, a swish of Petey the rescue peacock's tail drew his attention beyond the entry gate; black eyes returned his stare. He couldn't blame his little girl's favorite feathered friend for the strong hunch that settled in his gut.

Something was going down.

As he inspected the perimeter of the grounds, he pulled the cruiser to the far left side of the building—home to the gift shop and postage-stamp-size office.

At the back of the structure, a small apartment served as live-in accommodations for the resident veterinarian, vacant since the previous vet retired at the beginning of the year. In the interim, while the committee in charge recruited candidates with hopes to fill the opening, the town had been blessed when a mobile animal doc had agreed to commute each week and care for the preserve's wildlife.

Once more, he skimmed the fencing installed to keep the animals in, and trespassers out. Although Sweetwater, with its rich history as a frontier gold and silver mining town—population 1,025 at the latest census—was recognized for its low crime, on occasion he'd been called out for trivial grievances issued by the townsfolk. Like the citizen who complained about the garbage truck rumbling through the streets at 6:00 a.m. Or the discovery of a teenage prank that involved toilet-papering the statue of Sweetwater's founder erected in the center of Town Square.

But from the time the vandalism had occurred the previous year at the Sweetwater Bed & Breakfast—an historic icon since the town's inception by Constance Sweetwater in 1864—the station continued to receive more calls than usual categorized as suspicious. Even after the B and B vandals had been apprehended.

However, tonight's visit to the sanctuary hadn't been based on any tips. Jack's motive far exceeded those related to the line of duty. And that reason had become his whole life when Willow passed away. His fingers grazed the delicate band on his uniform once more, his heart warming as he pictured the cherubic face of their daughter, Josie, who fueled his purpose.

She adored the preserve and its animals, and had often enjoyed outings here with her mother. He would do anything in his power to help her retain those memories. And then one day in the future, he would present Josie with her mother's wedding ring—the symbol he wore like a second badge, although not one of honor.

Under the canopy of native trees that simulated the animals' natural habitat, scents from the sanctuary wafted through the open car window—hay and manure, and a hint of creosote, which was unusual at an elevation above 5,000 feet.

Then, a new sound. A thump that came from neither the pasture nor the preserve. It seemed to originate from within the building itself, on the side that accommodated the small clinic and vacant live-in quarters.

"Okay, now what's going on?"

A muted glow behind the window shades snagged his attention. Pressing a hand to his stomach in an attempt to quell the spasms, he again strained to listen as a fierce possessiveness stole over him. The community had fought tooth and nail for the preserve and sanctuary when developers had bulldozed their way into town, determined to raze several of the structures, including a handful of historic properties. *And to put in a strip mall, of all things.*

He snorted. While his shattered heart found no refuge on the property, he'd made a promise to his late wife that he would protect its interests for Josie. Running off the developers had been a no-brainer.

As he rolled the cruiser to a stop, its engine ticking, a loud crash penetrated the shroud of darkness. Pulse ratcheting up a notch, his fingers grazed the holster attached to his hip. Unlatching the door, Jack inhaled the earthiness and prayed that the element of surprise would be on his side to eradicate the vandalism tonight.

Especially as the last incident played across his mind, in which the gift shop had been broken into and ransacked, followed by a late-summer monsoon that had left a deplorable mess in its wake, ruining the evidence. After that, it had required many volunteer hours before the preserve could be reopened to the public.

A popular half-day visit for tourists and townsfolk alike, the nonprofit included educational demonstrations throughout the grounds. If the attraction possessed the funds to fulfill its mile-long wish list of activities and interactive programs, it would easily garner even more public interest. As it was, there was just enough in its coffers to care for the animals and maintain its limited paid staff.

And Sweetwater depended on tourists to boost

the small town's economy, whether it was the visitors who arrived to enjoy the laid-back lifestyle just ninety minutes north of Phoenix, or those romantics who wanted to see for themselves if there was any truth to the legend of Sweetwater—that there was something in the "sweet" water, and that true love prevailed.

Although Jack had experienced what he believed to be his sole opportunity at love, he wouldn't fault others who sought theirs.

The click as he leaned against the cruiser's door exploded like a belated Fourth of July firecracker set off in the stillness. Gut clenching, the last thing he needed was for a vandalism-in-progress to escalate into something more dangerous.

Josie's face flickered across his mind. The child had already lost one parent. Yet he could hear his late wife's words as if she was standing next to him... *You were born to be an officer of the law, Jack Wells.*

And Sweetwater—up until the developer had arrived the preceding year—remained a haven for its residents, with the majority of tourists behaving with respect.

His head pounded, the rash of vandalism a conundrum. The tampering at the bed-and-breakfast last year had been one thing; the random damage at the preserve another.

Another glaring concern revolved around retribution for repairs. Because if they weren't able to catch the culprits in the act, they might as well take up a collection.

Cowboy boots crunching on the gravel, his nerves twitched as he forced himself from imagining the worst. And then there was the catch-22.

The preserve could not afford to shut down, but it also couldn't risk driving away its patrons.

With painstaking steps, he crept toward the building, continually assessing the grounds. Besides the commotion just moments ago, the only other sounds had originated from the wildlife enclosures. And even though he knew the large rescue felines onsite were docile—which he'd learned from attending the afternoon feedings of the big cats with Josie—a growl from one of the tigers drove a shiver up his spine.

That's when he registered a different noise, like something scraping against wood. Angling his head, he felt for his pistol again, fingers lightly resting on the safety release.

It's now or never. With measured stealth, he stole around the side of the main building toward the rear with plans to startle the intruder.

His pocket buzzed and he stiffened.

If his cell phone's volume had been on, the ringtone would've alerted him to the caller's identity. But because he was off-duty, that meant it could be Josie. Although she was in good hands with the owners of the B and B—his friends Lacey and Persh—Jack had to be sure.

He reached into his pocket with his free hand and glanced at his phone. His shoulders settled, relief washing over him as a photo of his child filled the screen.

"Jose," he whispered.

The grating sound continued, as if a heavy object was being dragged across the hardwood floors on the opposite side of the wall where he stood deliberating.

Continue the surveillance, or answer the call?

He punched the connect button and pressed the mobile phone close to his ear as he dropped to his knees. The fragrance of loam pervaded his nostrils.

"Daddy, I mith you." He felt the tug on his heartstrings at the sound of Josie's little-girl voice, and the lisp that resulted from the loss of her two front teeth.

"Daddy misses you, too, Jose."

And then he saw it: a shadow shifting behind a small rectangular covered window. He uttered a quick "I love you" and straightened his legs.

But as he popped the device back into his pocket, he was nearly bowled over by the scent of lavender and the soft, yet unyielding figure that now squirmed in his strong grasp. Rooting his boots into the soil, he steadied himself, pulse tripping.

"I've got a gun!" the powerhouse in his arms shrieked, dark hair whipping across his face, lash-

ing him as her ponytail swished with each con-
tortion of her body, skin pale in the glow of the
motion-detector lights that illuminated the area.

Myriad emotions slammed into him, from confusion to fascination, to self-reproach as he held
her in his embrace—chalking them all up to his
botched surveillance. He released his hands from
the woman's bare arms, where gooseflesh popped
out in the night chill.

This spitfire was his vandal?

"Hold on, hold on!" He raised his hands in sup-
plication. "I'm with the law." He jerked his head
toward the badge pinned to his collar.

The idea of an accomplice not improbable, he
averted his gaze and squinted in an attempt to
peer inside the small apartment through the open
door. But then his attention swiveled back to the
woman in front of him. Her lab coat hanging open
over a T-shirt and jeans.

Oh, great.

Dr. Emerson Parker gulped several times, sucking in breaths of stolen air thanks to her run-in
with the solid wall she'd just barreled into full
force. Within seconds, she cataloged the Stetson
pushed low on his forehead, well-lived-in cowboy boots, a blazer and—as he'd indicated after
Emerson's threat—a metal badge etched with big
letters spelling out *Constable* pinned to his lapel.

Right beforehand, she'd been attempting to organize the quarters of her new home.

While the physical wounds that drove her to the small town of Sweetwater had blessedly healed, she'd sought out the preserve as her private sanctuary, fueled by prayer and hope that the healing properties of nature might help to mend the wounds still disfiguring her heart. The last thing she'd been expecting was to confront another human being before the morning arrival of staff and volunteers.

"This how you welcome all your new residents, Constable?" She focused on taking slow, deep breaths to regulate her pulse. Brushing at her wrinkled lab coat, a blush threatened as a result of her empty warning. In fact, she shuddered at the notion of handling a gun again, much less possessing one. But if she was reading appearances correctly, the Sweetwater lawman staring her down looked a lot more uncomfortable.

"I, um…" Shifting his stance, he palmed the back of his neck. "Suppose you wouldn't believe the welcoming committee sent me?"

She appreciated the constable's attempt at levity, but didn't miss the pink tint that crawled up his neck. His discomfort set her a bit at ease. After swiping a dusty hand on her jeans, she extended it toward him, a smirk tipping her lips.

"Hardly," she snickered. "But now that you're here, I could use some help."

While she'd been relishing the idea of soaking in the solace of the small town on her first night, she wasn't about to pass up an opportunity to engage the assistance of a strong and able body. Despite her familiarity with the dark side of human interaction—the kind that led to complications and heartache. Which was the reason she would be focusing all her attention on the animals in her care, while she navigated her own healing journey.

The constable's large hand enveloped hers.

"Emerson Parker, live-in vet." His palm was rough and his grip loose. Yet uncertainty propelled her to tug her fingers loose.

The last thing she needed was to let down her guard with a man. Not after her last relationship had left her badly burned. And by the expression in the constable's eyes, she surmised that he, too, was no stranger to fire.

He tipped his head. "Jack Wells." Scrunching his eyebrows, he noticed the plastic sack she'd been wielding upon their collision and retrieved it from the ground. "Uh…sure." He lifted the bag like it weighed no more than a balloon, then hitched his thumb over his shoulder. "Garbage?"

Without waiting for an answer, he headed in the direction of the dumpster a few yards into a clearing in back of the building.

"Thank you!" She heard the slight edge to her voice as she curled her fingers into matching fists and fought the urge to grab the bag from the constable's hands. Her defensiveness was a coping mechanism she continued to address, and all because of the fallout from her disastrous marriage and the impetus that drove her to the Sweetwater Preserve & Sanctuary. *To find healing.*

"Door's open," she called over her shoulder, then clapped her hands together before grasping the handle to the screen door of her little apartment, its hinges squawking and inviting the aviary inhabitants to elicit a fleeting cacophony of their own.

A whistle from the teakettle atop the compact stove in the well-appointed kitchen intermingled with the wildlife sounds. And not for the first time since her arrival at the preserve, she savored the peace within the shelter's confines.

After pouring the steaming water into a second cup—the first had slipped from her fingertips, ending up in shards she'd quickly swept away— she sprinkled jasmine-green tea leaves into a stainless-steel strainer, the sweet, soothing fragrance reminiscent of her childhood garden after a spring rain.

As she plucked an extra mug from the cupboard, the squeaking screen door alerted her to the constable's return. Yet, she couldn't squelch the tiny wince at his imposing presence. Another flashback from her past and the wounds that still required tending.

"I didn't think the new vet, er, you—" Constable

Jack covered his mouth with his fist as he cleared his throat "—was arriving until next week." His boots landed with heavy footfalls on the hardwood floor as he approached the corner bistro table.

Without forethought, she'd situated herself behind the furniture as a barrier of sorts. A window on the wall next to the seating area overlooked a copse of wildflowers no longer visible under the blanket of darkness.

"As you can see, I'm here now." She shrugged. "Tea?" Presenting a rectangular box on the palm of her hand, she displayed a vast collection of tea bags as she met the constable's shadowed blue regard.

Stetson still firmly in place, Jack thrust his hands in his back pockets and rocked on his heels, gaze wary. "Whatever you're having is fine."

She couldn't stop his guardedness from arousing her curiosity, but she refused to delve into the potential reasons for the constable's behavior.

Adding the same tea leaves to an antique silver ball she'd unearthed in one of the apartment's prestocked drawers, she dunked the orb into the water.

"Tell me, Constable, was tonight part of your normal rounds?"

Jack seemed to consider her question as he accepted the cup, then blew across the rising steam. All the while she covertly perused the five-o'clock shadow that dotted his cheeks, and the strawberry-blond hair that curled at the nape of his neck. The differences between Jack and her former husband practically jumped out at her. And beyond the physical—rugged versus cultured—she sensed the opposing personalities common between dogs and cats. Dependable versus unpredictable.

"Not sure how much you know," Jack responded. "And I don't want to scare you off." After taking a swig of the brew, he licked his upper lip before placing the mug on the coaster across from hers.

"I know about the vandalism." No sense mincing words since it had been one of her biggest considerations. But had she jumped from one unstable situation into another by accepting the job opportunity at the preserve? Her only consolation was to hope that now that she'd be living here full-time, the vandalism would cease.

As she sipped her tea, she continued to study the constable beneath lowered lashes. While less than thrilled with a man's presence in her new home, she welcomed his assistance with a few larger pieces of furniture. A shiver skittered along her arms. *Especially the electric fireplace.*

Jack shuffled his boots along the gritty planks, a tangible reminder that it still needed a good scrubbing.

"So what did you need help with?"

He swallowed a big gulp of the tea, and by the way he darted his eyes around the room and its austere, white walls, she had no doubt he'd prefer to be anywhere else.

She tracked his gaze toward the feminine touches she'd arranged in an attempt to transform the sterile space. So far, she'd unpacked colorful pillows and a blue hand-crocheted blanket—one of the few nonnecessities she'd packed upon fleeing her previous life—that were now piled atop the pull-out sofa that converted into a full-size bed. And a homemade quilt gifted to her by her Aunt Francine had been tossed over the back of a bistro chair.

Observing the worn furniture, she sighed. It would more than suffice, despite the fact it was a world apart from the pristine home she'd vacated a short while ago—one that had served as a showroom and perfect analogy to how she'd been expected to conduct herself. Or to pay the penalty.

Just like that, she grappled with a strong fight-or-flight response, her heart and respiration rates increasing. If Jack was to study her now, would he notice her dilated pupils? The telltale tremors in her hands? It was still too recent since she'd separated herself from danger, and too easy to forget she was now safe.

But was she?

She scrutinized the constable, his gun returned to its holster. Before she could respond to his question, a raucous sound emanated from beyond the clearing that flanked the building.

With just three strides, Constable Jack faced the screen door and Emerson flinched, her heart stuttering as he pressed his head against it and lifted a finger to his lips. He turned the handle, and the hinges remained blessedly silent.

After he slipped outdoors, she avoided unpacking the reason for her unruly pulse, instead blaming it on the obvious: the vandalism, and her different surroundings. And denying that its origins had anything to do with the noticeably wounded, yet ruggedly handsome constable.

So much for a laid-back, fresh start.

Despite the vandalism, however, her faith was grounded in God's provision going forward. Especially since her recent escape from her former situation—one that had given off warning signs from the beginning.

She scoffed in the silence. How naive she'd been by believing she could fix her fiancé once they were married. Yet it hadn't taken long before she learned the hard way that it wasn't her job to change hearts. And that what had originated as a gift could so easily turn into a curse—all because of her role as a fixer.

Because the wounded inevitably found a way into her life.

Case in point: Constable Jack, whose blue eyes revealed a deep valley verdant with wounds. It also hadn't escaped her notice that his fingers habitually touched the gold band he wore over his heart, adjacent to his badge.

There's a story there... The conspiratorial whisper was so clear it was as if her Aunt Francine was seated on the stool next to her.

And while she was happy to indulge the constable's nonverbal directive to remain quiet, she didn't intend to wait inside the apartment as he faced the unknown shenanigans taking place on the grounds.

"What better way to get acquainted with my new digs?" She tucked a long, errant strand of dark hair back into her ponytail. But as she pushed open the door, for the second time that evening she propelled directly into an immovable barrier.

"Oof!"

Without an ounce of hesitation, Constable Jack drew her into the full circle of his embrace, and she filed away the sensations as neither unpleasant nor threatening. Yet her eyes widened in surprise, perhaps as wide as saucers by the appearance of the constable's shadowed stare.

And even though her instincts prompted her to shove away from the man, the warmth that coursed through her veins resembled nothing akin to the fear she'd endured for so long.

"I thought I told you to stay put!" His voice was a low growl, much like the harmless chuffing from the preserve's felines. A puff of his breath hovered between them before it dissipated into the cool air.

She stiffened, an automatic response to the constable's tone. "I don't do well with orders, Constable." Her lips curled into what she hoped conveyed her displeasure. Well-versed with how the law worked—and not always in her favor—Emerson was treading on unstable ground by potentially hindering police matters.

Constable Jack's Adam's apple bobbed. Whether from irritation or some other emotion, she could only surmise.

"It's my job to keep you safe!" he insisted, the words tumbling out. "To keep the preserve safe," he quickly amended.

With sudden self-consciousness, she wriggled free from his hold, yet confused by his obvious reticence to end their standoff as his arms dropped to his sides.

Briefly closing her eyes, she repeated a familiar mantra. *It's not my job to fix him.*

She also didn't need him to assume the role of hero.

Straightening her spine, she gathered her resolve. "What happened out there, anyway?" She waved toward the darkness untouched by the security lights.

Jack adopted her example, regrouping. "I must've scared off whoever—or whatever—was out there."

Bowing his head, he sighed. "But now a little girl needs her daddy to read her a bedtime story."

She was caught off guard by Jack's pronouncement—the most he'd spoken in one sentence since his surprise arrival. Serving to remind her she knew nothing about him or his circumstances. *And it was in her best interest to keep it that way.*

Rubbing her hands over the length of her arms, the nippiness infiltrated the space between them and her weary shoulders sagged against the weight of her long day.

"Go home to your wee one," she whispered, light and heat spilling out as she pulled open the screen door.

"But you need help…"

From where she stood, she watched Jack's mental struggle that shifted between staying, and leaving. She knew that fight all too well. But her recent travels, and days—*correction*, months and years—of emotional turmoil came crashing down on her. She stifled a yawn.

"It sounds like you need it more than I do." Her words were infused with a meaning that extended beyond his policing duties.

Jack's broad shoulders dipped a couple of inches, the lines around his eyes diminishing. "I'll check back in the morning."

"I don't need babysitting, Constable." The timbre in her tone came off harsher than she'd intended. Yet she couldn't shake the sneaking suspicion that she'd just walked headfirst—literally—into a situation far more serious than her initial expectations. And not simply due to the vandalism at the preserve.

But because her oath to care for the wounded had proven it was not always a blessing. It could also be trouble.

Chapter Two

Unable to deny the sparks that had ignited in the presence of one feisty Dr. Emerson Parker, Constable Jack might very well describe his state of mind as twitterpated. The term borrowed from one of the countless cartoons his five-year-old daughter begged him to watch with her. Yet the heels of his boots would not budge until he heard the telltale click from the lock on Emerson's side of her door. But it was the mass of fleeting emotions clouding the doctor's eyes that haunted him. Dark orbs wide with fear, yet guarded.

Spitfire was right.

He grunted as he recalled his original assumption that Emerson was the culprit behind the vandalism. What he hadn't counted on, however, was his confusing feelings toward the new veterinarian.

He slapped his Stetson against his thigh before shoving it on top of his head. He would prefer to start over on a better foot with the doc before vacating the premises, but he'd been at the sanctuary to perform his duty. Not to tango with the newest resident in town.

No more and no less.

Spinning on his heel, he stayed behind to take

a final look around. By way of an indirect path leading toward his cruiser, he remained hidden from the view of a casual observer. Or that of a potential trespasser.

Because even though the noise he'd heard while inside Emerson's apartment could've belonged to one of the dozens of onsite rescue animals, it also might've turned out to be something—or someone—else. Truth be told, he held little hope of singlehandedly catching the vandals in the act. Especially if they were dealing with more than one perpetrator.

He massaged the knot at the base of his neck, the heavy burden of his role as the town's constable weighing him down. Yet at the same time, he thrived on his vocation. He would even go so far as to consider it a divine calling to serve and protect.

But more often than not lately, he faced increasing doubts about his ability to do his job. Fleetingly, his fingers hovered over the gold band pinned next to his badge, the ever-present tangible reminder of his failure.

As he continued, he passed the aviary's netted habitat, noting that most of the rehabilitated and rehomed winged residents had tucked in their feathers for the night, while a few cackles bordered the paved walkway.

Next, he crossed in front of the massive, caged-in arena where volunteers educated daily visitors on the feeding habits of their resident tiger couple, each rescued from different circumstances. From what he'd learned, Tony had originally resided at a Midwest zoo that closed down due to misappropriation of funds. And instead of returning the large cat to the wild, Tony had been rehomed at the preserve. Tina, on the other hand, had arrived on the grounds due to life-threatening injuries at the hands of poachers.

His phone pinged just then and he recalled his earlier promise to read Josie a bedtime story—the dropping temperatures emphasizing the elapsed time since ending their call.

Stealing a quick inspection of the bear cave, confident that nothing appeared amiss, he hurried toward the petting zoo and his daughter's favorite area. After examining the kangaroo "krib" and hyena haven, and detecting nothing out of place, he smiled at Josie's desire to name each of the rescues.

Thanks to a mother she'd spent hours with at the preserve. Until it was no longer possible.

"Not now." Hand on his pistol, he rounded the remaining enclosures. Confident everything was in order, he returned to the spot where he'd begun. Sensitive to Doc Parker's defensiveness, he'd remained covert as he surveyed the area, but he still had a job to do and a promise to keep. Regardless that he'd been unable to keep Willow safe, or that the vet objected to his interference.

After hopping behind the wheel, he buckled up

and set course for the Sweetwater Bed & Breakfast. But not before one final glance at the building that contained the clinic and small apartment, both now silhouettes in the darkness.

He checked the emotions incited by the woman he pictured beyond the dimly lit window. But if misery loved company, as the saying claimed, he was convinced Doc Parker was also dealing with her own set of issues. He had sensed it within her dark, wide eyes; like a deer caught in the headlights—a common occurrence he'd experienced up close and personal along the curving mountain roads countless times.

Yet despite the feelings that simmered beneath the fragile surface of his heart, he snubbed the very idea of getting involved with another woman in any capacity. Especially since he'd been unable to protect his one true love from the cancer that claimed her life and left their daughter motherless.

Swallowing hard as if chunks of gravel had taken up residence in his throat, he pulled into the front parking lot of the historic bed-and-breakfast and exited his vehicle. Softening his steps, he passed beneath the white wooden trellis climbing with lavender-star flowers. While the blooms didn't have much of a scent, the moniker conjured involuntary images of the raven-haired vet.

He paused before rapping lightly on the screen door, willing his mind to the present as he waited under the muted glow of the porchlight. Swiping one hand over his whiskered jaw, he said a silent prayer of thanks for his friends; Lacey and Persh had been a blessing upon Willow's diagnosis, and had remained one ever since.

Before sliding into that murky rabbit hole of what-ifs and sad memories that would sometimes chase his thoughts, the door to the inn swung open. Brightening the evening with her smile, Lacey Sweetwater—aka, Mrs. Lacey Pershing—stood across from him, her fiery copper hair aglow. The very trait that her husband, Councilman Drew Pershing—Persh to all who knew him—had teased her about as kids and dubbed her with the nickname, Red.

"Sorry I'm so late." He stepped over the threshold as Lacey welcomed him into the foyer.

She brushed his forearm lightly, conjuring another woman's touch and his differing reaction.

"No apologies necessary, Constable." Placing her index finger over her lips, with a toss of her head Lacey indicated the living area, where his flaxen-haired daughter lay on an antique love seat.

His heart squeezed as he gazed at Josie; the single most precious gift his late wife had gifted him.

"Someone fell asleep while Uncle Persh was reading." Lacey chuckled.

"I got tied up at the preserve again." Absently, he craned his neck to peer into the dining area, where gourmet breakfast was served daily to overnight guests.

"He just stepped into the kitchen for a bedtime snack." Lacey winked, then retrieved the tote he packed for Josie on the evenings that duty called, a practice that had escalated since the vandalism had picked up at the preserve. But during the day-time, his daughter attended the church's preschool in the downtown area, close to the precinct.

At Lacey's offhand comment about her hus-band's whereabouts, the evening's internal and external friction melted and his mood lightened. Of course, it was no surprise he might find Persh in the kitchen, especially since his best friend had ended up marrying the great-great-great-grand-daughter of Sweetwater's founder and original proprietor of the inn. Which meant Persh was granted 24/7 access to Lacey's gourmet cooking, as well as the sweet and savory sundries stocked by Annie's Confections & Catering.

Persh interrupted his musing, practically barrel-ing into Jack as the swinging door that separated the industrial-size kitchen from the dining area slapped his friend on the back. A chocolate-chip cookie was wedged into the corner of his mouth, his eyes laughing.

"Drew Pershing." Lacey swatted her husband's arm with a playfulness that Jack envied.

Persh winked, then shook his friend's hand. "Hey, buddy, you hiring extra help at the station?"

He snorted. "You got any candidates who want to work for nothing that I'm unaware of?" After accepting the tote that Lacey handed him, a souvenir from the preserve, he slung the cloth strap over his shoulder.

Persh ran his fingers over his sandy brown hair and the goatee on his chin before leaning his hip against one of the dining-room tables. "I wish."

The other man's eyes assessed Jack, as if perceiving a glimpse of the turmoil that remained from the aftermath of his confrontation with Emerson.

Speaking of. "I thought the new vet started next week?"

To avoid Persh's probing gaze, he crossed the wooden floor, then scooped a still-slumbering Josie into his arms. Traces of baby powder and sugar cookies enveloped him, along with an intense protectiveness that hitched his breath in his chest.

This time, he would not fail to serve...and, most importantly, to protect.

"You mean Dr. Emerson Parker?"

It's as if he could feel Persh's eyes bore into his back. He didn't need his buddy to read anything more into his brief introduction to the vet. But the councilman was sharp. Jack had witnessed with his own two eyes as Persh had battled it out with the developer that tried to shut down the B and B the previous year. Not to mention his friend's persistence in winning Lacey Sweetwater's heart amid the snafu with her grandparents' will.

But that was a whole other story.

"Yes… Doc Parker." He met Persh's discerning observation head-on.

The councilman pushed away from the table to fish another cookie from the glass container in the entryway—the one Lacey kept stocked for their guests—then popped it into his mouth before brushing his hands together.

A few crumbs fell to the floor, and Jack didn't miss the look Lacey shot her husband before she grabbed a stuffed lamb that had tumbled to the floor and tucked it into Josie's fuzzy blanket.

"You two get home safe now." She smiled at him, a compassionate expression in her eyes, then spun toward the staircase that led to the owner's suite. "Before I retire, can I interest you in a glass of iced water, Constable?"

He reflected on the legend of Sweetwater and the promise that there was something in the sweet water—the myth couched within the history of the B and B. In fact, he might've given it credence if he hadn't met and fell in love with Willow a few towns over.

"I'm good, but thank you again for everything." He moved toward the door, welcoming the downy softness of his daughter's white-blond hair that tickled his neck as she snuggled against him.

"It's always our pleasure." Lacey hooked Persh's attention. "Please lock up."

With a few long strides toward his wife, Persh

kissed the top of her unruly locks, causing an ache in Jack's heart. Yet when the vision of a dark-haired spitfire in a lab coat flared up, he was afraid his friend would detect the tug-of-war hidden beneath Jack's Stetson.

"She asked if it would be okay for her to start early," Persh said as he joined Jack by the door. "That one's got a story, her reasons for choosing Sweetwater." A thoughtful look crossed his face. "I pray she finds what she's searching for."

He understood the draw of the small town, which was the main reason he'd never considered making a life elsewhere. Even after he brought Willow back to his hometown, he reckoned they'd marry and raise a family here. And one day he'd retire and they'd grow old together. But not all stories ended in happy-ever-after. Not like the ones Josie was fond of.

He snapped himself from his reverie. "I'm just glad someone's onsite full-time." His fervent hope was that the vandalism would stop now that the apartment was occupied.

Would Persh end the conversation? Or attempt to wheedle out Jack's opinion with regard to Doc Parker?

Josie elicited a cooing noise, prompting the councilman to pat him on the back.

"Take your girl home and get some sleep. You look awful."

"Thanks a lot," he grumbled. Exiting through

the door Persh held open, with his buddy chuckling, he tried to tamp down thoughts of the new vet. He could revisit them another time, if ever. Especially since he only had room for one female in his life. And that was a pint-size, five-year-old little girl named Josie Wells.

Yet that didn't mean he took lightly the responsibility of watching over the entirety of Sweetwater. All due to the role that had been thrust upon him as a young boy when his father—Clint Wells—had deserted him and his mother. Meaning that Emerson Parker, as the newest resident of Sweetwater, was included in the jurisdiction in which he served and protected.

With a drowsy Josie tucked into her car seat in the back of his cruiser, he traced her face and pledged once more to do just that.

No more and no less.

Although the latter oftentimes proved the biggest challenge.

As he turned his cruiser onto historic Main Street and swerved into a vacant parking spot, the cottage he and his late wife purchased loomed ahead.

Had it always appeared uninviting…or just since he'd erected the wall around his heart?

After the constable vacated Emerson's apartment, a strange sense of loss consumed her—the absence of his larger-than-life presence left her feeling out of sorts. And she wasn't sure how to process that, because it had been a long time since she'd felt safe with a man other than her father.

Her motive for seeking comfort in Sweetwater had been to heal her emotional wounds, the scars that ran deep from a toxic marriage. She'd hoped to close the door to her past as she immersed herself at the preserve, and cared for the wounded rescues without a voice. The voice she'd finally used too late.

Tidying up the small space, she placed her empty mug and Jack's half-empty cup of tea in the sink. In the wake of his absence, a trace of pine and muskiness lingered. She inhaled as she stared into the distance.

"What have I gotten myself into?" Rinsing soapy water from the cups, she set them on a mat to dry, then hung the dish towel before returning to the few boxes left to unpack. Her lips curved into a smile as she recalled the constable's consternation as she coaxed him to help. His awkwardness had stirred an inquisitiveness.

Already weary from the day's events, she decided to retire early. Before her move, she'd been employed in a big city where she performed her job with ease. And although she had no reason to believe her duties at the preserve would be any different, her background didn't include quite the diverse bunch of wildlife.

While most of her former patients fell within

the general classification of dogs, cats, birds and equines, at the preserve she'd be working with a new set of clientele. The likes of which included lions, tigers and bears. *Oh my!* She chuckled. "As well as peacocks, hyenas and a llama!" She grinned again.

It would be unlike anything she'd ever experienced. But that's what she needed—the polar opposite of the "perfect" life she once lived. Rather, perfect in the eyes of those acquainted with the public personas of Aaron Parker and his veterinarian wife. They had surely been the couple to be envied.

Except that behind the closed doors of their estate—furnished with a housekeeper and driver—she'd compared herself to a prisoner. Aaron had even forbade her from leaving their home without his permission, unless work had warranted it. And if she'd ever dared to deviate from the house rules, she had paid in private.

Beginning to tremble again, she pressed a hand to her chest to still her racing heartbeat as vivid memories of her last night with Aaron rattled her insides.

Then, without warning, images of a strawberry-blond lawman attired in cowboy boots and a custom-fitting Stetson, with a shiny gold band pinned to his shirt next to a badge, replaced the dark images.

As seen through her eyes, Jack came across as

a man dedicated to serving others, perhaps to the denial of his own needs—evident by the way he grappled between staying to help her, or leaving for his little girl.

Realizing she'd been lumping thoughts of the constable alongside her painful, broken past, she groaned. New memories surfaced, those of Aunt Francine, her father's only sibling. The woman who'd helped raise Emerson as a young girl after her mother had passed away. Her aunt had always loved a good story, and no doubt there was one lurking beyond the brassy sheen of that ring. As she pictured Aunt Francine, a woman of strong faith, her pulse calmed.

If only she'd paid better attention. Heart clenching, the carnage of her shattered marriage was still fresh. But it hadn't been the broken commitment she attributed to the ache. Rather, it had been the subsequent loss she lived with each day.

The one from which she had yet to escape.

Because the abuse she'd endured by Aaron's hands stole far more than her self-worth, for which she carried the blame. Involuntarily, her fingers fluttered against her now-flat abdomen, an action that occurred less often since that fateful night mere weeks earlier.

Returning to the bistro table where she and Jack had shared tea, she pushed up the window that looked out over the small garden of wildflowers swallowed in the shadows. For a few minutes, she basked in the magnified sounds surrounding the preserve, then closed and locked the window. Devoid of the constable, the space seemed to shrink in on itself.

Unable to stop replaying their interaction, she cringed as she recalled her defensiveness when Jack had brandished his badge. Yet, he'd backtracked and altered his intent from protecting her to safeguarding the preserve. She tried to ignore the nagging in her spirit and instead justified her behavior because of how her ex-husband had treated her.

But that didn't mean all men were created equal. Her previous counselor had reminded her of this truth several times before she'd escaped from her perilous home life.

Although Jack had likely disregarded her careless words, he had done nothing to warrant anything less than her gratitude. Even still, she'd gone from residing under her father's roof to married and living with Aaron. From her childhood home to a marital prison. Not only were her skills rusty when it came to the opposite gender, but she had no intention of getting involved with another man for any reason.

She inhaled sharply, pushing aside her negative thoughts as she studied her living area. A tiny bathroom was located on the other side of the modest kitchen that was furnished with a microwave, dorm-size fridge and freezer, and a two-burner cooktop stove. The pull-out sofa took up the far wall, along with a compact coffee table and an ornate changing screen; a heavy armoire and portable electric fireplace flanked the opposite wall. Sweet and simple.

Everything will work out. The promise washed over her. Welcoming the peace that enveloped her, she allowed herself additional musings that revolved around a certain constable.

Regardless of her own experiences, she sensed that Jack was unlike any man she'd known…although she wouldn't be surprised if he ranked second to her father, who'd raised her alongside her Aunt Francine. The latter had instilled in her the courage to stand up for herself. *Even though it had cost her everything.*

She brushed at the wisps of hair on her forehead, as if swatting at a pesky horsefly. After switching off the overhead light, she padded toward the tiny bathroom to wash up.

If only I'd paid more credence to my dad. Learning how to discern the good guys from the bad would have weeded out Aaron Parker. His charm and good looks had reeled her in, but it had been the wounds he'd harbored that had sealed the deal. Those that she thought she could heal.

But after having traveled down that road once, she had no need to revisit it. Animals were both safer and more predictable, in her opinion. She anticipated employing her horse-whisperer abilities on the wildlife at the preserve, "a gift from above," as her Aunt Francine had described her talents.

History had proven, however, that at some point in time, the scarred and broken would land on her doorstep. Whether friend or, in her ex-husband's case, foe.

The room now canopied in darkness, she settled under the thin comforter. Tugging at the crocheted baby blanket from the foot of the bed, she closed her eyes.

Please guide my interactions tomorrow, and help me to find healing and wholeness in this place.

And then her brash encounter with one tall, handsome, and wounded officer of the law snuck into her prayers. *And help me to make amends.*

All while keeping the man at arm's-length distance, of course.

Who was she trying to fool? She felt safer knowing that the constable kept watch. She offered up a petition for him as well. For whatever caused the sadness that dulled his eyes. And for his little girl—the bright light that transformed his entire face at the mere mention of her.

Another child filtered through her mind and heart. A little boy who would never take his first breath. Or stare into his mama's eyes with the dark gray gaze inherent in all newborns.

Hovering between that puzzling state of wakefulness and slumber, she tamped down the evening's events. But not before she pictured the gold band next to the constable's badge and what it might imply alongside a walled-up demeanor shielding the sorrow that clung to his rough edges. Not to mention his hunched shoulders, as if he bore the load of an entire community. All of which made it easy to forget her silent pledge to remain uninvolved.

Sunlight streamed between the blinds hanging over the window through the top half of the apartment door. New and distinct noises filtered into Emerson's consciousness, serving as her wake-up call. Wishing she'd turned on the electric heater, she shivered in the cool air. As she nestled deeper beneath the blankets to enjoy a few extra moments, she created a mental list of that day's tasks.

First, she planned to get a feel for the land where she now lived and worked, and to meet the staff and volunteers who helped run the preserve. Next, she hoped to venture into town when feasible to acquaint herself with the community. Because even though she craved the quiet of the sanctuary, she also longed to make connections.

And somewhere along the way, perhaps she'd figure out how to properly thank the constable for doing his job.

Chapter Three

No more and no less.

Jack snickered. He didn't have to look far to see the outcome of his poor attempts at juggling job responsibilities, as well as managing his home and family of two, which had revealed his ineptness at single-parenting. If not for the helping hands of those closest to him and Josie, they'd be existing on boxed macaroni and cheese, and soup from a can. Not that that was the worst thing.

"Daddy, can you put pretties in my hair?" Josie skipped into the sunny kitchen decorated in yellows and white, that Willow had chosen when they'd purchased the historic home. Although he'd barely made ends meet on his salary at the station when they'd first married, as soon as he saw how much she'd adored the homey cottage, making the investment had been a no-brainer. And now he was raising Josie in a home established on the foundation of love.

He twisted his face into a goofy smile as he stooped to Josie's eye level, which made her giggle in delight...and reveal her missing front teeth. He held out his hand to accept the hair ties that dangled from her fingertips. After pressing a kiss atop her bedhead of flyaway hairs, he grabbed the brush she carried, then shook his head. Would he ever get the hand of these girlie things?

"Scoot up here." He helped her stand on a wooden chair and started brushing out the knots when his pager went off.

"Ouch, Daddy!" Josie clapped a hand to her head.

He winced, slowing his strokes as he peeked at the pager lying face up on the table. Councilman Pershing's number flashed on the screen. It must be about the funds for the preserve. Jack had leveraged his friendship with Persh—stopping just short of begging—to put in a good word with the town's council. In particular, he needed the funds for additional man power to assist with surveillance at the preserve.

He still held out hope that a live-in vet on the property would slow—or, better yet, stop—the vandalism. In the meantime, he watched over the town's interests by day as best as he could, while maintaining his vigils most nights at the preserve. But work aside, his biggest difficulty of late was keeping things straight on the home front. Especially when he continued to revisit thoughts of Doc Parker.

He released a sigh. Even though he never intended to avoid Emerson, despite his routine surveillance, he'd made no effort to check in on her since their run-in a few nights earlier.

"I'm thirsty, Daddy." Josie faced straight ahead

but screwed up her little face to make eye contact with Jack.

"Hold on, Jose." He parted her hair down the middle, then gathered one section in his large hand before binding it with an elastic band. He grabbed a carton of juice from the fridge, then started to pour the liquid into a plastic cup.

"Daddy, not lemon juith!"

Josie's giggle and lisp snapped Jack from his musings. He groaned, plunking the bottle of citrus juice onto the counter, its contents splashing. Not the fresh-squeezed OJ—compliments of Lacey Sweetwater—that he'd had in mind.

One more piece of evidence that he could barely keep his head above water. Josie might find his minor mistakes silly, but if he didn't get his act together soon, one of his slipups could prove dangerous. That's why the extra funds for the station had to be approved.

"I'm sorry, baby girl." He emptied the sour liquid back into its container and rinsed Josie's cup before refilling it with orange juice. He handed her the drink, then proceeded to put the finishing touches on the pigtails that Josie favored.

"Can we stop at Mith Annie's before 'kool?" Josie's bright blue gaze sparkled, wide and expectant.

While she shared his identical eye coloring, her fine white-blond hair matched her mother's, and each year he claimed his daughter resembled

Willow more than the last. A way that helped to sustain his late wife's memory, along with the photographs scattered throughout the small cottage.

His hand drifted near his collar, and the wedding band he wore pinned next to his badge, before forcing himself to the task at hand. "Only a quick stop, baby girl."

After wiping down the counter with a wet rag, he grabbed one of the lunches Lacey stocked him up with. His buddy was sure blessed when Lacey agreed to be his wife. Speaking of Persh, he still needed to return the page—no doubt about the latest council meeting he'd missed. Both he and Josie had overslept, not to mention they'd fallen into a pattern of late drop-offs at the preschool. And even though the staff had been understanding, it wasn't fair to his daughter—or the other children—to make it a habit.

Maybe the part-time business manager at the bed-and-breakfast—Marie Michaels—who divided her time between the church and preschool offices, would appreciate an assortment of Annie's sweet confections. It couldn't hurt to invite equal parts goodwill and leniency for his rash of tardiness.

Or, better yet, why not charm the town council? He tilted his head and guffawed at the idea of law enforcement bribing city officials in the name of hiring more help.

"Why are you laughing, Daddy?" Josie climbed off the kitchen chair before dropping her empty cup in the sink.

"Your daddy's just being goofy." He stuffed the lunch bag in Josie's backpack, then helped her pull the sack over her shoulders. Today she'd chosen a pretty, long-sleeved pink dress covered in bluebells, a pair of blue tights and slip-on sneakers. They were even on the correct feet. Tugging on one of her pigtails, he locked the cottage behind them. *I guess I'm not doing too bad after all.*

Although that hadn't been the sentiment Persh had alluded to all week. In fact, upon Jack's arrival to pick up Josie from the B and B for the third or fourth time in as many days, his buddy had scolded him for burning the candle at both ends. Which had become par for the course as a single father.

He pushed play on a CD compiled of songs the kids had sung at last summer's vacation bible school, persuading Josie to sing along, while he returned to mulling over his dilemma.

He certainly couldn't maintain the status quo much longer. Or it was just a matter of time before something more serious than mixed-up juice and missed council meetings could happen. Which was the reason Jack needed additional man power stat. And he depended on Drew Pershing's clout as newly elected town councilman to be his saving grace.

As he drove toward Annie's Confections & Catering, conveniently located across from Town Square, a question he'd agonized over during the past few years resurfaced. While Willow had been alive, had he been too focused on his job to serve and protect that he'd missed the signs of her failing health?

Because if that was true, an earlier diagnosis may have resulted in a treatment plan to stop the cancer before spreading. He'd spent countless nights on his knees, mining for clues by replaying their last months together. But since Emerson showed up, she'd begun to consume his thoughts. And the overwhelming feelings of protectiveness, he simply justified as a heightened sense of duty. The simplest way to justify the feelings she'd stirred when she'd barreled into him.

"Daddy… Daddy!"

In the nick of time, Josie's voice wrenched him from his musings. Stomping on the brake, the cruiser jerked to a stop at the red light.

Heart hammering, he turned in his seat to check on Josie. The expression in her blue eyes mirrored another set that were darker in contrast, but no less wary.

He shook his head, blood boiling over his blunder. "You okay, Jose?" He swallowed back his angst as he placed his calloused palm against her soft cheek.

"Yeth," she answered, voice small.

"I'm so sorry for scaring you." Twisting back to face the road in front of them, he proceeded with extra caution once the light changed to green.

"Can we thtill go to the bakery?"

He chuckled, pulse returning to normal. *Ah, the resilience of a child.* While Josie often talked about her mother, she'd begun to forget bits and pieces about their times together. But other devout Sweetwater women had stepped in to carry out the biblical directive to keep watch over the orphans and widows. It was always a beautiful sight to witness their love and compassion to his daughter.

Josie would not lack a female presence in her life—a blessing beyond any gratitude he could express. Especially when he had no plans to fall in love again. That horse had been put out to pasture…or however the saying went.

He scoped out the curbside parking adjacent to Annie's. With the arrival of autumn and the cooler temperatures, many of the regular tourists remained in warmer climates, which left coveted space available in front of favorite local hangouts. Annie's had been at the top of the list since the bakery opened the previous year and expanded into a catering side.

Annie was the daughter of Captain David Greene, a firefighter killed on duty, leaving her mother to raise the young girl alone. The baker had arrived in town to start over—a common denominator among numerous Sweetwater transplants.

An image of Doc Parker wormed its way back into his mind's eye as he pulled into a vacant spot directly in front of Annie's. He unbuckled Josie, then hoisted her into his arms, where she tilted the brim of his Stetson and planted a sloppy kiss against his cheek. As he hip-checked the door closed, she strung her arms around his neck, causing his chest to swell with equal parts love and pride.

Stepping over the curb, he glanced at Town Square, its patch of manicured lush green grass situated across the two-lane street lined with giant sequoia, Colorado spruce and alligator junipers, as well as aspen.

The bronze statue bearing the likeness of Sweetwater's founder, Constance Sweetwater, rose skyward in front of the courthouse steps that led into another of the town's historic buildings. It was the hallowed space where the town conducted its important business—from voting about encroaching developers, to whether or not funds would be allocated to the law-enforcement department.

"Daddy, look!" Josie pointed toward a gap between Annie's bakery and another shop that sold gear for day hikes—a popular pastime enjoyed by enthusiasts who explored Sweetwater's numerous forested trails, including those along the banks of the lake named after the town. A reservoir formed by a dam on a creek located south of town in north central Arizona, it also boasted areas for picnicking, fishing, boating, volleyball and horseshoes.

After setting Josie on the sidewalk, he crouched to peer into the shadows.

"A dog!" Josie edged closer.

"Stay back, Jose." He tugged on the hem of her dress. "We don't know if it's injured." *Or worse.*

Sudden inspiration struck. He could swaddle his jacket around the pup for easy transport to the preserve and sanctuary's clinic, where it could receive care. *Delivered by Doc Parker.*

If the dog turned out to be a stray, Emerson would nurse it back to health. And if no one claimed the pup, he might make a good watchdog. Except that rescuing the dog also meant the risk of once again letting down his guard in Emerson's presence. Was he prepared for that?

He inched toward the mangy mound of fur, then glanced at Josie.

"Run into the store and pick out your treat, while I try to help this guy." Although he didn't have high hopes, he couldn't ignore a creature in need. He straightened so he could peel a few dollar bills from his wallet, then slipped them into Josie's hand.

"Okay, Daddy. He looks schweepy now."

No need for him to disagree with his daughter; and the sooner she chose her goody, the sooner he could get her to preschool. And the pooch to much-needed help.

Keeping an eye on both the dog and Josie, he watched his daughter yank at the door to Annie's, which made the bell chime, and the home-baked aromas from lemon bars to gourmet granola to caramel and chocolate-dipped apples wafted out to the street.

Confident that Josie was in good hands with Annie, he put his full attention on the grungy pup. Shrugging out of his jacket, it didn't take much to coax the sick-looking hound into the folds of cloth.

"There now, big guy, I know just the person to fix you up right as a summer rain."

Gently, he deposited the pooch on the front seat of the cruiser before jogging the remaining steps to the store. With his focus on the dog, and getting his child to school, he failed to notice the person on the other side of the door who bent down to pint-size level.

That is, until a whiff of lavender assaulted his senses.

The chimes tinkled in Jack's wake, and at the same time Annie emerged in a flurry from the kitchen.

"Constable Jack!" Both Annie and Emerson exclaimed in unison, Jack's wide eyes and slack jaw a clear indication of his surprise.

It had been Emerson's first opportunity to venture into town since her arrival, so she'd taken the advice of preserve volunteers to swing by the charming bakery during her morning break.

A few minutes before Jack had rushed in, Annie—the proprietress of the bakery she'd already met—had been removing a batch of fresh-baked bread from the oven, while she'd been scanning the rows of delicacies before a little girl with white-blond pigtails slipped through the opening and skipped over to a glass case containing a variety of cake pops.

At the sight of the child, Emerson's heart squeezed, her loss still fresh. Memories of a little boy who would never experience the joy of homespun sugar melting on his tongue, or sticky frozen yogurt dribbling down his chin, had briefly flashed through her mind.

"It'th juth me, Mith Annie!"

Oh, what an endearing lisp.

"So what's good here?" She'd joined the little girl, glancing up to see if a guardian hovered nearby. When no one appeared, it reaffirmed to her the town's reputation as a haven and the refuge she'd sought.

The girl had gazed up at her with a gap-toothed grin that explained her lisp. But it was her eyes that sparked an electric jolt straight to her sensible-soled shoes.

Because they were duplicates of the icy, bright blue eyes that belonged to Constable Jack Wells.

Whom she was now staring at, his jaw working as if he'd been struck speechless.

"Daddy, ith the puppy okay?" The little girl launched herself at Jack and he scooped her into his arms.

The man certainly appeared as taken aback as Emerson felt at running into each other again, if the flood of color that crept up his neck meant anything. His Stetson appeared off-kilter, too, revealing a head of cropped strawberry-blond hair that curled at the ends. He righted his hat as he addressed the child with kind eyes and a gentle voice.

"The pup is safe and sound in my car. Did you pick out your treat?" He deposited the child on the tiled floor and she started running, her pigtails bouncing.

Stopping midway, she twirled to face Emerson. "You're pretty!" Then she took off for the colorful selection of cake pops.

Emerson smiled at Jack. "She's a sweetheart."

Jack's eyes gravitated toward his wee one, who was reaching into the case to pull out a sundry.

"Josie's a good girl." His Adam's apple jumped as he spoke, a pensive note tingeing his tone. But as they waited in silence, and he continued to observe his daughter, his posture relaxed.

She detected the pride in Jack's voice, equal parts tenderness and protectiveness. But now her tongue seemed to stop working, and she couldn't remember why she stood in the middle of the bakery. Which might just prove her initial reaction toward him had been more than a fluke.

Not to mention the endearing bond between father and daughter, which was a big part of the constable's story. Compliments of a little birdie named Lacey Sweetwater.

She spotted the gold band pinned next to Jack's badge, the concrete evidence of grief that lingered around his edges.

"What's this I hear about a puppy?" She chose to blame her conflicting thoughts and erratic pulse on low blood sugar. "I am a doctor, you know."

Winking, she adopted a quirky smile. Somebody needed to lighten the mood.

"You can help the dog!" Josie scurried over and pulled on Jack's pants leg with one chubby hand, a paper bag clutched in the other. "Daddy?"

But Jack appeared speechless again, reminding Emerson of how he'd been a man of few words that night at the preserve.

And even though there'd been no additional surprise visits from the constable, she'd suspected his police cruiser—headlights dimmed— had been patrolling the perimeter of the grounds after hours.

"That's a good idea, Jose." Jack snapped out of his stupor. "The injured pup's in my car."

She returned to her professional demeanor. "I can meet you at the preserve."

Just then, Jack's pager went off. After glancing at the screen, he reached for his cell phone. "Let me make this call real quick."

"Daddy, I'm going to be late for 'kool." Josie jumped up and down, still gripping the paper bag.

"One second, Jose." Jack held a finger to his lips.

Without a second thought, Emerson stepped in. "So, what are you learning in school?"

The concern etched into the child's expression made her appear older than preschool age, which was no surprise considering the loss the child had suffered. But, for all intents and purposes, so had Josie's mother.

She swallowed the tears that threatened, her own loss the result of poor judgment. Had she heeded the warning signs associated with her ex-husband, she could've prevented the tragic outcome.

"My numberth." Josie's singsong voice interrupted Emerson's dark musings, the little girl's attention focused on her father.

"That leaves me in quite a bind, Councilman Pershing." The pitch of Jack's voice had escalated before he abruptly ended the call then swiped off the Stetson to run a hand through his hair.

"Unbelievable!" He stared out the large window at the streetscape beyond.

"Daddy, you didn't thay goodbye!"

As if Jack suddenly realized his whereabouts,

his neck and cheeks became even pinker. "You're right, Jose," he said, making eye contact with the child. "I lost my temper with Uncle Persh and used bad manners."

The defeat Emerson detected in his blue eyes had turned them into a dull gray. Yet she could identify all too closely with how it felt to have your back pinned against the wall.

And without seeing it coming, the wounded had gained a foothold in her life once again.

She'd learned a bit of the constable's story when Lacey had stopped in at the preserve and sanctuary to welcome her on her first day. The man was nursing hurts that ran as deep as a sinkhole and as wide as a valley. It would be foolish for her to get close with her own still raw.

Sighing, she straightened her back. She was in no position to help shoulder the problems of another human being. Not to mention the misery that her soft heart for strays and the injured had brought her.

Jack reached for his daughter's free hand. "Sorry about that. You said I could bring the dog to the clinic?"

"Yes, I'm heading back momentarily." Might this present an opportunity to make amends from the other night? Jack's phone call with Lacey's husband seemed to put him in a bind—perhaps news he hadn't been prepared to hear. "Anything else I can help with?"

He popped his Stetson back in place, tension lines framing his mouth. A mouth she had no right to focus on. Jack Wells was the last person she needed to be concerned about. Never mind the emotions he stirred.

Because she refused to put her heart at risk.

Jack stepped toward the door, oblivious to her spiraling thoughts.

"Only if you know someone looking to work for free." He pulled a deep breath and released it with a half chuckle. "Because it looks like that's the only way I'll get help."

Jack's words confirmed her original assessment that he carried the weight of the small town squarely on his broad shoulders. She could relate to that, too. But for her, it had been the burden of an abusive relationship that had culminated in the loss of her son shortly before her arrival in Sweetwater.

"Never mind." Jack fixed an unconvincing smile on his handsome face. "See you in a few." As father and daughter exited the bakery, Jack hollered, "Thanks, Annie!"

Emerson turned her attention toward the younger woman, who'd kept to herself behind the counter while Emerson and the constable had conversed. *What must she be thinking?*

"Do you need some help?" Annie joined her and nodded toward the glass case.

But a sliver of an idea had begun to take shape

in her mind. One that might just be an answer to prayer.

"More than you know!" She chuckled at the double meaning.

Annie placed a gentle, flour-smudged palm on her shoulder and squeezed. "You're in good hands." She pinned her with a deliberate look.

Safe in the hands of the constable? Or the townsfolk in general?

Either way, a quiet life in Sweetwater was looking less promising by the minute. Because a pint-size, pigtail-sporting little girl with bright blue eyes—and her Stetson-wearing, law-upholding and wounded father—had somehow found a fissure in her heart.

And she wouldn't be surprised if it was too late to do anything about it.

She raised her eyes to the heavens. *Very funny.*

"If you need to talk, you know where to find me." Annie's blue-gray eyes regarded her with compassion.

The other woman had no idea how much her implied offer of friendship meant to Emerson. Because outside of her work with animals, Aaron had forbidden her to spend time cultivating more than casual acquaintances. But now, between Annie and Lacey, she was eager to navigate the rare and beautiful gift of friendship.

"What do you suggest?" Tempted to choose a certain little someone's favorite cake pop, she struggled to make up her mind. She grimaced. Apparently, that referred to more than just picking out a dessert.

"Honey, you can't go wrong with anything that's made of sugar."

Without warning, a sensation she'd long forgotten welled within her until it overflowed in the form of a full-on belly laugh. "Taste and see that the Lord is good!"

Both ladies dissolved in fits of giggles as the door chime announced another customer. A rugged man dressed in full firefighter garb stepped across the threshold and into the store.

"Hey, Josh Rogers." Annie waved, a shy smile tilting her lips.

The man's presence proved as commanding as Constable Jack's, and just as comforting.

"Hi, ladies." Josh's gaze strayed to Annie and lingered.

Emerson stifled the urge to laugh again. It was blatant that the firefighter was smitten with the baker. But then, sudden recognition lit his golden-brown eyes when he noticed her doctor's scrubs.

"You're the new doc?"

"I am." She accepted his firm handshake. "Emerson Parker."

"Aw, shucks." The crease between his eyebrows deepened. "I hate to break up the party, but I just got word the preserve was struck again." With frustration, he smacked his large hand against his thigh. "No one's hurt though, just another mess."

In broad daylight? Her mind raced. The preserve! She'd promised to meet Jack and the dog. Opting to forgo her treat, she offered a quick thanks and an apology before rushing out the door.

Once on the sidewalk, the inkling of the idea she'd begun toying with—the potential answer to prayer—coalesced right there on the edge of Town Square.

It completely railed against her commitment to remain unattached, however. It would also mean jumping feet first into circumstances that would, in all likelihood, prove a greater threat than the vandalism.

The very real threat to her already delicate heart.

Chapter Four

~~

After Jack checked Josie into preschool—arriving under the radar just as the tardy bell peeled—he slid behind the wheel. A whimper from the passenger seat begged for his attention. The dog's sad, brown-eyed glower radiated between hope and despair.

"I get it, boy." He scratched the tattered hound between his ears before shifting into gear. He checked his mirrors before rejoining traffic, then headed toward Sweetwater Preserve & Sanctuary.

Now what? His heart uttered the question, while his mind still digested the news from Councilman Pershing. So much for getting the needed help. He'd hoped some extra dollars could have been funneled into the station's coffers, but the lack of funds meant that his work patrolling the preserve would continue. Off the clock.

Yet that arrangement wasn't working too well. Just as he and Josie had arrived at the preschool, the scanner on his dash had picked up a report from Josh Rogers that vandals had made another hit on the preserve, which required him to make another report. But he would stop at the clinic first to deposit the mutt that had already weaseled his way into Jack's good graces.

Although he hadn't questioned his choice to rescue the dog, it had been Josie's heart for animals and her connection to the preserve that fueled his motivation. The same reason he took on surveillance of the sanctuary and his justification for additional help at the station.

But the latter was no longer an option. He slammed his fist on the steering wheel as he pulled onto the familiar unpaved road. *So much for a place of refuge.*

The very space Emerson had chosen for her sanctuary had become a thorn in his side, as well as a source of guilt whenever his mind wandered to thoughts of the vet, as if he betrayed his late wife's memory.

Except that it was more than an attraction. It was like he'd been asleep these past few years and going through the motions before something, or someone, had opened his eyes.

But until he could eliminate his culpability, the wedding band would remain a part of his uniform, and his impetus for doing what he had to do. As well as the reason for avoiding relationships with women.

After he parked near the clinic entrance, he retrieved his lightweight bundle from the passenger side. "You're going to be good as new." His murmurs blended with the animal's whimpers.

As soon as he entered the clinic, Carley, who split her time between working as clinic receptionist and gift-shop clerk, welcomed them into a modest sitting area, where Doc Parker was waiting.

The contrast between Emerson and Willow was like a punch to his solar plexus. While the vet exuded an air of confidence, his late wife had possessed a shyness. And with her dark hair and eyes, as well as olive skin, Emerson reminded him of their Native American ancestors. By contrast, Willow had been fair and waiflike.

"Hey now, bring him over here. Nice and easy."

Her soothing tone washed over him, along with her floral scent. Reining in his thoughts, he placed the stray on the exam table and stepped out of the way.

"Okay, now let me see what we're dealing with."

Emerson crooned to the pup, who seemed as mesmerized by the doctor as Jack was becoming.

"Thank you for bringing him in. I understand if you need to deal with the latest…issue." Emerson flashed a brief smile, brown eyes professional, yet sincere.

Although he felt as if Emerson had dismissed him, he grappled between staying and leaving. "I'll check back before I head out." He tipped his hat and pivoted on his heel.

Entering the gift shop, he approached the counter, where Carley was now stationed at the register. A handful of patrons browsed through the merchandise for sale, much of it handcrafted by locals.

He lowered his voice. "Can you point me to the damage?"

"Sure thing, Constable. Just head over to the bear's enclosure."

He raised a hand in thanks, proceeding toward Buzzy's den. Several years ago, the preserve's staff had rescued the injured black bear and relocated it from a small, unincorporated town northwest of Sweetwater. At the time, the bear—named by Josie—had been foraging a wild berry patch when illegal hunters shot the animal for sport.

Thankfully, a video that bystanders forwarded to authorities led to the arrest of the perpetrators. And ever since his arrival at the preserve, Buzzy had been spoiled with all the wild berries, bananas and mangoes he could consume.

"Unreal." His jaw dropped at the sight of the lair swarming with flies, scattered rotten fruit and a disoriented-looking black bear. "I don't get it."

Unless it wasn't about the damage. Could there be an ulterior motive behind the vandalism?

He retraced the events from the previous year. How the developer had steamrolled into town, determined to acquire several of the historic properties by nefarious means. Although the offenders involved had ultimately been held accountable for the isolated sabotage, that didn't rule out a connection between the two incidents. Was it an attempt to have the preserve shut down?

After filing away that angle for further consideration, Jack snapped quick photos of the mess just as a couple of volunteers arrived with a trash bin and cleaning supplies.

Once he circled the grounds, he returned to the clinic to check on the pup…and as an excuse to borrow more time with Emerson. Because despite his conflicting emotions, the woman's nurturing persona did wonders to soothe his rattled spirit.

"I'm glad you're back." Emerson's dark eyes landed on Jack. "You brought our little fellow in just in time. The poor thing was malnourished and dehydrated."

Observing the purple shadows that smudged the tender skin beneath Emerson's large eyes, his pulse tripped at her reference to "their" dog. Tamping down the what-ifs that had been plaguing his fitful sleep at night, he shoved his hands into his front pockets.

"It was Josie that saw him." Maybe now would be a good time to broach the topic of Emerson keeping him as a watchdog once he was healed up.

"Please tell Miss Josie that he should feel like his old self very soon. And she's welcome to say 'hi' anytime."

Emerson's lips curled upward. Oh, yeah, he may be in big trouble all right. Especially if he starts believing in those what-ifs.

"Any ideas about the latest?" Emerson waved a hand toward the direction of the grounds.

"I haven't the foggiest." He scratched his forehead. "And without the funds to hire full-time security onsite…" He bit his tongue. It wasn't his place to air the station's dirty laundry, but a lack of security could jeopardize her safety. "Honestly, I don't know how much longer I can keep the powers that be from closing the preserve."

"What?" Emerson didn't hide the dismay evident in the fine lines between her eyes, her tone agitated.

Because in addition to concerns about her safety, the preserve served as her job and her home, as well as her refuge. And if she lost it all, it would be on his watch.

"I can help." Emerson clasped her hands in front of her, a resolute expression on her face that matched her stance.

"Excuse me?" He yanked off his Stetson, wringing it between his fingers.

"Let me help with the surveillance." Conviction laced Emerson's words.

He felt the proverbial brick wall against his back, once more. Not only was it clear that her arrival had done nothing to thwart the vandals, but the attacks had also escalated. The town council would demand answers. And without them, the preserve would fold.

Regardless, he couldn't evade the veterinarian indefinitely. As much as he wrestled with the emotions she stirred, he had learned that God's ways were not always his ways. And to fulfill his vow to protect his late wife's beloved preserve, the only logical choice was to accept Emerson's offer.

Of course, that would require an indeterminate amount of time together, and a risk to the one thing he'd safeguarded for the past three years.

His heart.

He traced the rounded edges of the band pinned to his collar. And for the first time, rather than his heart clenching, it felt more like an unfurling. As if his prayers for help had been answered, even if that help came from a raven-haired spitfire with eyes the color of rich, dark chocolate.

Once she blurted out the undoubtedly unorthodox offer, Emerson observed the myriad expressions that ran across Jack's rugged face. From the moment he'd left her apartment that first night, shame at her behavior had swept through her, and she'd prayed about how she might apologize to the constable. And after witnessing his phone conversation with Councilman Pershing, the answer came quickly. Because the preserve and sanctuary were important to her, too. With Jack's hands tied, she might be the answer to his troubles.

Never mind that she'd be adding her quandaries to the equation. And assisting Jack would mean working together. Closely.

While she might be privy to a few of Jack's inner wounds, he remained in the dark as to her own struggles and vulnerability, and the conflicting emotions triggered by his nearness. Namely, the promising image of what a healthy relationship between a man and woman could look like.

But her instincts had failed her once before.

She squeezed her eyes shut briefly, willing the dark thoughts to flee.

I'm forgiven. Those two words soaked into her spirit. It wasn't the accountability she battled pertaining to the loss of her child, but her willful involvement with Aaron. One day, perhaps she would find the strength to forgive herself. And to open herself up to a relationship again.

But it was not that day.

Nor was the constable in any position to reciprocate.

He could prove a good ally in the future should a lawful need arise, however. Especially with what she'd learned from Lacey about the developer's involvement the previous year, and now with the vandalism at the preserve.

Still waiting for Jack's answer—whatever it might be—she vowed to protect her bruised and battered heart. Even if it was more difficult each time they were together.

"What's it going to be?" She inhaled the faint scent of Jack's musky aftershave.

"It's unconventional."

She exhaled as she imagined his mind working behind those blue eyes. He put his Stetson back on, then, the action evoking images of an old-time sheriff from a classic Western. He just needed to swap out his cruiser for a stallion.

"But the sooner we catch the culprits, the better our prospects to keep the preserve running."

Of course, that had to be the deciding factor. The property served as more than a place to work and live. It was answered prayer—a refuge for her, and no doubt countless others.

Even during her short time in town, she'd observed a community that helped carry one another's burdens, proving that true love prevailed—which was a legend in itself, according to her jaded opinion. But wonderful to believe in. *Except for herself.*

Helping Constable Jack, and the preserve, was the right thing to do. Whether or not that meant enduring close proximity to the handsome, and oftentimes brooding, officer of the law.

"Is that a yes then?" Were the wheels turning in his mind like that of a hamster's as he tried to find a loophole?

Except that from what she'd gleaned from Lacey, the Sweetwater Preserve & Sanctuary meant just as much to Jack, if not more. And if she could serve a small role in maintaining his late wife's memory for both him and his daughter, it might also help to absolve her remaining guilt. And help her heal.

Jack clasped his hands together, mirroring her. "When can you start?"

A tentative smile slid into place and she chuckled. "Just tell me when to toss the white lab coat and replace it with dark attire."

Jack's shoulders loosened as a sigh shuddered through him. A picture of relaxation? Or was he relieved? Either way, she liked the new look. Maybe a bit too much for her good.

"Let's talk details when you're off duty…er, work." Jack pivoted toward the clinic's entrance, where another pet owner had just entered, carrying a large cage containing a bird screeching at the top of its lungs.

"Hey, I want to catch them, too." Her words traveled the distance between them as Jack approached the exit. She was on his side. And that of this community, where she longed to find human connection after being deprived from it for so long.

He stood stock-still an extra beat, a gulf seemingly separating them. But then something shifted. A charge in the air, as if finding common ground bridged the gap.

"I know," he replied with his less-is-more flair for conversation. "I'll call you." And then he disappeared.

As it had that first night, his absence affected

her by creating a strange emptiness. Soon, though, she was preoccupied with treating one patient after another throughout the afternoon. From the bird with a damaged wing and ill temper, to their resident bear, who was sulking after his temporary transfer to another enclosure so his den could be scrubbed down. Buzzy was not a fan of change.

Of course, who was? Yet it was within the midst of change where people often experienced growth—during times of stretching and pruning. Not always through the most pleasant of experiences, which oftentimes yielded the best harvest.

In between appointments, several of them drop-ins, Emerson checked on her new charge, which brought on additional thoughts of Jack and his blue-eyed munchkin.

"I'm locking up for the night, Doc," Carley said, interrupting her wayward musings.

Glancing up from the computer screen where she was entering the day's reports, she offered the college student a smile. "Thank you, Carley. Enjoy your evening." Carley was studying to become a veterinarian as well, and Emerson made a concerted effort to support the younger woman's endeavors whenever she could.

While waiting to hear from Jack, she reminisced about the first time she'd discovered her gift for healing, and compassion for the wounded. She had been right around seven years old when she and her father had stayed at a family friend's log cabin not long after her mother had passed away. As her dad had pulled muck from the gutters along the eave above the back deck, he accidentally bumped a bird's nest wedged there.

She could still hear her cry of anguish as the baby bird fell from its home, minuscule wings attempting to flap haphazardly, its beak opening and closing as if calling for help.

Afterward, with the utmost care, she'd gathered the tiny fuzzy creature and placed it in an empty tissue box for safekeeping. For some time, her dad had helped her feed it sugar water with an eye dropper, gently squirting some on the side of its beak, enticing it to open its mouth and swallow.

Her dad had warned her that their intervention might hinder the mama bird from returning to its offspring. But after a couple of weeks of nursing her injured feathered friend, father and daughter had returned to the cabin and replaced the nest nearby the log building, along with the baby bird. Maintaining a daily vigil from a nearby vantage point, Emerson had prayed for the mama bird to return.

A soft smile played across her face as she pictured her young self. And how she'd eventually been dubbed the Animal Whisperer by her veterinarian colleagues. The incident with the baby bird had also been the first time she'd witnessed the power of prayer. Sadly, it took decades for her to understand that not every prayer of hers would result in a happy ending.

As she closed down the computer programs, the phone line to the sanctuary flashed red for an incoming call.

"Sweetwater Preserve & Sanctuary, how may I help you?"

"Dr. Parker?"

It only took four syllables for her heart to register the caller's identity, sending a pleasant thrill careening through her veins.

"This is Emerson. Are you on your way?" Could Jack hear the beat of her pulse across the connection?

"Change of plans."

And couched within those three words, she absorbed both his frustration and weariness. As if they were her own.

Chapter Five

At the sound of her voice, Jack's heart rate sky-rocketed. He would address these confusing re-actions in prayer. But first he needed to square away the surveillance plans.

"Turns out I can't make it to the clinic." When he'd picked up Josie from preschool that after-noon, he'd been directed to the nurse's office. Her normally bright eyes were dull and her cheeks were flushed with fever. Since losing her mother, his gut clenched anytime she exhibited signs of illness. Although surveillance needed beefing up at the preserve, his child always came first.

"I hope everything is all right."

The concern in Emerson's voice melted his de-fenses.

"Josie's got a fever." He could've reached out to Lacey to watch his daughter—and had considered it. But Josie's little arms clinging to his neck as he'd carried her from the nurse's office to his ve-hicle had solidified his decision to keep her home. He'd been entrusted as her father—the role just as serious to him as that of constable.

"I can come to your home."

He heard the tentativeness in Emerson's tone. *But was that what he wanted?* The ache in his stomach intensified. It was one thing to spend time with her on official duty. But to invite her into the space he'd shared with his late wife?

Yet he couldn't deny his need for help.

That's when he was reminded of the story—or perhaps an old wives' tale—of the man trapped on the roof of his house during a flood. The man had prayed for help. Soon a person in a rowboat showed up and shouted to the man on the roof, "Jump in! I can save you."

The stranded man replied, "No, it's okay, I'm praying for God to save me." So the rowboat continued.

Next, a motorboat came by. The fellow in the motorboat yelled out, "Jump in! I can save you." The stranded man repeated his earlier statement and the motorboat also left.

When a helicopter hovered over the man and the pilot shouted down, "Grab this rope and I will lift you to safety!" the stranded man gave the same reply and the helicopter flew away.

Of course, the tale always ended in the same way, with the water rising above the rooftop, and the man drowning. And when he arrived in heaven, he asked, "Why didn't You save me?"

To which God responded, "I sent you a rowboat and a motorboat and a helicopter, what more did you expect?"

"That works!" He wasn't going to be the man

who refused help—divine or otherwise. Even if that meant welcoming Emerson into his home.

After he'd conveyed his address and directions, he began tidying up the cottage. As he straightened the pile of magazines on the coffee table, outdated reading material he had yet to find the time or energy to flip through, he tried viewing his home through the eyes of a stranger. From the cozy decor that Willow had chosen to furnish their home, to the pale yellow walls and white trim with accents of teal blue and coral. She'd always sought his opinion before each purchase, and without fail, he'd extended his blessing to decorate however she saw fit.

His heart squeezed. Even though he wished he'd been more involved in the process, he was grateful that he and Josie enjoyed the fruits of her labor. And, in the end, it wasn't the paint colors or throw pillows, but the walls and surfaces peppered with preserved memories—as well as the love and laughter contained within its walls—that had transformed a house into a home.

With quiet footsteps, he entered Josie's princess room, where his little girl had fallen asleep after changing out of her school clothes. His chest swelled at the sight of her bow lips, long lashes resting on her chubby pink cheeks. Placing the back of his hand against her forehead, he confirmed that her skin no longer felt warm to the touch. *Thank You, Lord.*

Always one step behind, he returned to the kitchen to finish loading the dishwasher with that morning's breakfast dishes.

Once he and Josie had gotten home, he'd re-heated a batch of frozen chicken-noodle soup from Lacey. But his little one had conked out on her bed, so he stuck the soup in the fridge then swapped out his on-duty attire for casual wear.

He glanced at his denim and flannel. Maybe he should have retained his official garb. He certainly didn't want to give Emerson the wrong impression. *But she was the one who offered to meet here.*

The chimes at the front door alerted him to his visitor. No need to second-guess himself now.

And thanks to his erratic pulse, which was racing along his nerve endings, he didn't even need to check the peephole.

Throwing open the front door, the air whooshed from his lungs at the sight of Emerson without her customary lab coat and the stethoscope that dangled from her slender neck. Yet she wore the same dark braid draped over her shoulder, wispy tendrils framing her oval-shaped face.

His throat constricted and he wiped his clammy hands along the sides of his pants. Could he be coming down with the bug Josie had brought home from school?

Or, more likely, it was his response to the woman facing him.

"Um…are we meeting on the front steps?" Emerson's full lips quirked in obvious amusement.

Warmth prickled the length of his neck and he managed to swallow the lump as he held the door open wider.

He didn't have the privilege of second-guessing her offer to help without money from the town council. "S-sorry…come in."

The fragrance of lavender enveloped him as Emerson squeezed past into the entryway.

Following his new "partner" into the living area, he observed her survey of the furnishings. "It's small, but it works." He held his breath, waiting for her reaction.

Emerson slowly rotated full circle, brown eyes sparkling. "It's charming."

And when she graced him with a smile, the wall erected around his heart shrunk a tiny bit more.

"Hi, Mith Dr. Parker." Josie tiptoed across the threshold of her bedroom, curiosity written in the curve of her eyebrows. Thankfully, the brightness had returned to her eyes since her fever had subsided. Dressed in her favorite princess nightgown, her little feet were bare and her white-blond hair smooshed from sleep.

As he watched his daughter, he almost missed the imperceptible flash of grief that registered in Emerson's soft gaze, which she quickly disguised with another smile, this time directed at Josie.

"Well, hello, Miss Josie. And, please, call me Em."

Emerson appeared at ease in the presence of his child, which made sense in light of her gentle nature and tenderness toward animals. The way she'd cared for the stray dog was tangible evidence, in his book, that the town's new vet had found her calling.

"How'th the puppy doing, Mith Em?" Josie padded into the living area toward Emerson, who squatted down to Josie's height.

"You found our boy right in time." Emerson's fingers had been intertwined in prayer, and she released them to tweak one of Josie's mussed-up pigtails. "Now what's this about you being sick?"

"Daddy thaid my fever ith all gone." Josie yawned. "Do you think I can name the puppy?"

Emerson chuckled, a throaty sound that curled Jack's toes in his socks.

"I think he would like that very much. When you feel better, why don't you come and visit him?"

Emerson's eyes snapped to Jack—her brown-eyed gaze nearly knocking him off his feet with a questioning look.

"That is, if your daddy says it's okay."

Did she think he'd keep Josie away from the preserve? Despite his reluctance to hang out at the sanctuary himself, he'd always respected Josie's connection to her mother by fostering early memories of their trips.

"Can I, Daddy?"

Hope colored Josie's cherubic face, her wide eyes melting his heart. "Of course, you can. Now let's fill a cup of water and get you to bed. Miss Emerson and I have business to discuss."

Josie wrinkled her nose. "Can you read me a book, too?"

"A quick one." He struggled to deny his daughter at times. Although he did his best not to spoil her, he went above and beyond to ensure they spent quality father-daughter time together. Which left little time for himself at the end of the day, and often caused him to fall asleep as he said his bedtime prayers.

And for so long, those prayers had focused on the ache of loss and how to move forward. But since Emerson had arrived on the scene, this newest ache he experienced centered more on what he might be missing in his life.

"Can I get you anything before I tuck in this munchkin?" Boosting Josie onto his shoulders, his eyes roved over Emerson's flowered skirt and the billowy orange top that complemented her darker skin.

It was at that moment he realized how much the woman had brightened his days. And that he might end up over his head with the doc if he wasn't careful.

Emerson's lips tilted upward, the armor around his heart slipping further. *Yep, way over.*

"I'm good, thank you."

"Okay, make yourself at home." And despite his earlier argument with his conscience, he meant those words from the bottom of his softening heart.

"Take your time."

Emerson pursed her mouth, causing his to grow dry as she blew a kiss toward his daughter.

"Sweet dreams, Josie."

"'Bye, Mith Em!" Josie pretended to catch the kiss as she waved her pudgy hand.

As Jack crossed into the bedroom, then, and lifted Josie from his shoulders, he glimpsed Emerson making her way toward the picture window that flanked the back wall of the kitchen and eating area. In the daytime, the view beyond revealed a modest yard teeming with the crimson-red blooms of autumn sage that was common in the High Country, as well as Colorado spruce, juniper and mountain maple native to the area. Although eager to get back, he welcomed their routine bedtime activities to gather his faculties.

"I like her." Josie yawned as he brought the chenille blanket to rest under her chin. He took in the canopy princess bed, an extravagance he'd purchased after she'd graduated from her crib. One of several attempts to compensate for what he perceived as his deficiency as a single parent.

Although his best buddy, Persh, didn't have to tell him twice that a princess bed was no substitute for Jack's presence and his daily involvement in Josie's life.

Which was the biggest reason he'd accepted Emerson's help. Because once the vandals were apprehended, he'd be able to stop dividing his after-hours time with his daughter, who didn't deserve to be on the losing end.

"She looks like Pocahontath," Josie said.

Funny, that same idea popped into his mind thanks to spending hours with Josie watching her animated video on continuous loop. Which meant he could also recite the soundtrack by memory.

He laughed, choosing a book from the bedside table. "I think so, too." Jack planted a kiss atop his daughter's white-blond wisps, her cool skin a balm that allayed his fears.

Midstory, she fell asleep. He clicked off her lamp, then left her door ajar before returning to the living area. Emerson stood near the fireplace studying a photo of Willow displayed on the mantel.

His thudding heart at the sight of her was no surprise. But rather than feeling guilty because of his reaction, it was something else entirely that he wasn't ready—or prepared—to analyze. Because the emotion might prove more threatening than anything he'd ever faced as the town's constable.

Within a foot or so of reaching Emerson's side, her shoulders stiffened, and she pivoted then recoiled. One hand shot in front of her face as if to shield it, and her pupils enlarged as terror blanched her complexion. For all intents and purposes, it appeared as if she was poised to ward off an attack.

But within seconds, her gaze lowered, thick lashes shuttering her inner chaos from the outer world. And that meant him.

Her pale cheeks pinkened, perhaps out of embarrassment at her overreaction. It was as if he'd just witnessed a different side to her. Rather than the confident, yet sometimes defensive woman she appeared to be, if she'd admitted to seeing an intruder, he would've believed her.

Could her reaction be a clue to what drove her to Sweetwater, and that still troubled her today?

"Hey, I didn't mean to startle you." Jack lowered his voice, palms raised in front of him as he backed away.

Emerson had been admiring the happy faces commemorated in the black-and-white photos arranged on the walls and lining the mantel. But then the fine hairs on her arms had lifted with a suddenness that demonstrated her parasympathetic nervous system was alive and well, her fight-or-flight response actively engaged.

Hands dropping to her sides, she gulped a few times before pulling in calming breaths on counts of six, exhaling on counts of eight. It was a technique her counselor had taught her to cope with her panic. She examined Jack's eyes, grateful they were filled with compassion and concern rather than pity.

"I-I'm sorry, I…" She longed to explain herself. But then shame sluiced through her, because she'd missed the obvious signs with her ex-husband. Worse yet, she'd remained in the abusive marriage even after discovering he'd duped her.

Until that last night when they'd been together and she lost their unborn child. Not long before she finally fled from Aaron and life as she once knew it.

She willed her pulse to settle, the memories threatening to drag her under. She told herself it was not her ex-husband standing in front of her. It was Constable Jack, the town's law-enforcement officer who possessed a servant's heart. A good man, and a good father.

Except that she shouldn't need to apologize for her response, either. Not after years of second-guessing the triggers that would set off Aaron. And even though her outward bruises had healed, counseling sessions had taught her that there's no timeline for inner healing. Another reason the mere notion of getting involved with another man was nothing short of a risky proposition.

"So about the surveillance." Jack nodded in the direction of the kitchen, where a sheet of paper and pencil were visible on the round table.

Emerson's shoulders relaxed at the shift in topic as well as his discretion. As she followed Jack into the eat-in kitchen, she skimmed his casual attire and noted how he appeared more approachable, softer around his occasionally gruff exterior. A combination that did nothing for her resolve.

Mouth suddenly parched, she blew at a wisp of hair against her cheek. Taking a seat at the table, she averted her attention from the flannel shirt that tapered from broad back to narrow hips, where it tucked into his denims.

"I haven't had dinner yet… Interested in leftovers from the B and B?" Jack pulled a container from the freezer and held it toward her, forcing her to make eye contact.

Just then, her belly emitted an unladylike rumble and she couldn't stifle a giggle fast enough. "Does that answer your question?"

Jack chuckled, the fine lines at the corners of his eyes visible. He busied himself at the microwave, the situation that had transpired in the living area swept under the rag rug beneath his stockinged feet.

She only wished it could be that easy to sweep away her regrets—the memories that plagued her dreams.

Soon the room filled with a spicy aroma. "That smells delicious. Can I help with anything?"

Jack's hands stilled for a fraction of a second before he began dishing up two plates of what appeared to be enchiladas. "Nope, I'm good." He added a premade side salad he'd grabbed from the crisper and filled both of their glasses with ice water.

She hiked up her eyebrows then took a swig of the brew. "Is this the same water that Lacey serves at the inn?"

Jack set the plates on the scarred wooden table. "One and the same." He smirked. "I take it you've heard about the legend?"

Based on how her own love story ended, she refused to believe in the myth that couples who drank the aquifer's sweet water ended up together. Although she appreciated the romanticism that fueled the legend tracing back to Lacey Sweetwater Pershing's great-great-great-grandfather, Constance Sweetwater, and each of the Sweetwaters in between.

She nodded. "Is that cynicism I hear in your tone, Constable?"

"Not cynicism. Just realism." He took a seat before bowing his head.

She didn't push for more of an answer. Instead, she followed Jack's lead, saying a quick prayer over their meal and little Josie's healing. And for the man situated across the table. Because whether he would admit to it or not, she had no doubt he needed healing, as well.

They tucked into their meals, then, accompanied by the occasional clinking of silverware, and intermittent snippets of conversation about the weather and Emerson's job at the clinic.

When he'd cleaned his plate, Jack pushed it aside and wiped his mouth with a napkin, then placed it on the table. "So how are you with a gun?"

One minute she'd been covertly studying the constable, and the next he'd dropped a bombshell. Sputtering on a piece of chicken that nearly lodged in her throat, she didn't even attempt to conceal the panic in her expression.

"Absolutely not!" She backed up her words with a firm shake of her head, long braid whipping over her shoulder.

But Jack appeared unaffected. "Then you'll need to carry pepper spray. Okay?"

Swallowing a few times, her pulse steadied. She was no stranger to guns; she'd even fired one before pledging never again to touch a firearm. Whether or not it had been used in self-defense, the memory remained.

Because a gun had saved her life, but not that of her child.

She would do anything if she could relive the past. But she could only control her decisions going forward. Taking a second sip of the sweet water, she cleared her throat.

"I can do that."

It began to drizzle as Emerson inspected both sides of the intersection before crossing. When she'd left the clinic earlier, intending to stop by the farmer's market, she'd inadvertently forgotten to grab her umbrella. Now she tried to "run between the drops," a funny saying of her father's that would make her laugh as a child whenever the two of them got caught in the rain.

As she splashed through a couple of potholes pooling with water, her mind rehashed the first of several nights of surveillance duty, where they'd been set up at opposite ends of the preserve. She and Jack had carried walkie-talkies on loan from the station.

"You okay?" Jack's whisper had thrummed in her ear.

"Ten-four." A nervous giggle had escaped and she slapped a hand over her mouth.

"Good, now keep alert, Doc." Seriousness laced his tone, reminding her of the reason for their covert surveillance.

The sky had soon turned to gray and she blended into her surroundings as night fell. The minutes had ticked by slowly and without event. And then Jack's voice had crackled across the walkie-talkie.

"So when did you know you wanted to work with animals?"

That had been an easy question to answer. "When I helped nurse a baby bird after it fell out of a gutter." She'd smiled at the memory. "When did you know you wanted to be a constable?"

The silence that had met her ears made her

wonder if they'd lost their connection. But then his voice had sounded so close, as if it were possible to reach into the shadows and touch him.

"It was just me and my mom when I was growing up."

He'd paused, as if considering how much he'd wanted to share. "I got the hang of taking charge and knew I wanted to be a lawman, and now that it's just Josie and me…"

Emerson had willed him to continue, while at the same time, she'd been unwilling to take that step herself.

"Let's just say she's my reason for doing what I do."

She'd released a breath then, as she'd slid down the wall of the enclosure that housed the preserve's reptiles. Jack's devotion to his daughter was an attractive quality that she couldn't deny. And one that made it all too easy to let her guard slip.

At least her willingness to use pepper spray had proven to be a moot point, as they hadn't witnessed any signs of tampering, or breaking and entering, during their subsequent vigils.

Yet at the light of some mornings, the discovery of onsite wreckage, albeit minor, would indicate the vandalism would have to be transpiring during the wee hours.

The staff would inform her after first rounds, fueling Jack's agitation upon each call she placed to the station. No doubt partly due to the town council breathing down his neck over the ongoing debate pertaining to the status of the preserve. Even his best friend, Drew Pershing, who was on the council, proved to be powerless.

And should the preserve shut down—either temporarily or permanently—Emerson would lose her home and her livelihood. Yet even worse than that in her mind would be the displacement of countless rescues.

But as her Aunt Francine often reminded her, there was no need to borrow trouble for tomorrow, when today had enough of its own. Shaking the drizzle from her hair, she stepped through the doors to the market.

From the moment she entered the makeshift space, her senses were assaulted with a plethora of scents from ripe produce available for the choosing, the sight a welcome contrast to the gloomy weather.

From what she'd learned from Annie at the bakery, with the cooler temps rolling into town, the market had recently moved its vendors from the Sweetwater Community College's parking lot into one of the campus's auditoriums, where it would remain until midspring.

"Doc Parker?"

Spinning on her rubber-soled sneakers at the sound of a man's voice, she recognized Lacey's husband striding toward her.

"Hello, Councilman Pershing!"

"You know you can call me Persh." He extended his hand, a big grin on his face revealing a crooked front tooth.

She returned his greeting and winked. "And you can call me Emerson."

"Touché." The councilman chuckled, then picked up a ruby-red tomato, tossing it in the air a few times before placing it into the overflowing basket. "How's the surveillance going?"

While she had no reason to doubt Persh's intentions, she didn't feel it was her place to report on official police matters.

"Still hoping for a breakthrough." At some point, she assumed Jack would either add to his report or fill in his friend between juggling his varied hats—in addition to the ever-present Stetson.

As if he hadn't heard her, Persh continued. "You may already be aware that Sweetwater hasn't dealt with vandalism since that developer showed up last year."

"That's what Jack...er, the constable mentioned." She felt the heat rise to her cheeks at the slip of Jack's given name.

But the councilman's attention appeared to be pinned on the past. "Was quite the shock to discover the culprit behind the shenanigans was former Councilman Spagnoletti's nephew."

That name.

She'd heard it before. It could be several years ago now. But where?

From a few booths away, a man hollered Persh's name.

"I've got to run." The councilman turned to wave at the person who hailed him. "But my wife gave me explicit instructions if I ran into you to extend an invitation to the B and B's annual Thanksgiving dinner." He started backpedaling in the opposite direction. "Please say you'll come or my bride will somehow fault me." He guffawed. "Just bring yourself—Lacey always prepares enough to feed half the town."

"Tell her I'll be there!" She watched as Persh clapped an older gentleman on the shoulder. She smiled to herself, an invitation for the holiday gathering a lift to her spirits. But the name that niggled at her conscience cast a shadow over the exchange with Lacey's husband.

Spagnoletti.

A quick peek at her cell phone reminded her she had only a few minutes before she needed to return to the clinic. Before this afternoon, she'd had little time to do any shopping or much of anything else. Not since working days at the clinic, and evenings on surveillance with Jack. The latter of which—although regularly separated by the animal enclosures—had been accompanied by an increasing camaraderie.

During many of those occasions, she'd been

tempted to share her story with him, but that feeling had been quickly replaced by an overwhelming rush of humiliation. The thought of the light dimming in his bright eyes once he discovered her culpability had been too much to consider.

Although it wasn't pity she feared. It was the horror reflected in her own gaze that kept her from divulging her secrets.

Willing away the dark musings, she quickly paid for her bag of produce and returned outdoors to find the rain now pouring in sheets. Unable to run through the drops, she could only take extra care to avoid the puddles. After tossing her groceries on the back seat, a flat tire all but mocked her.

"Ugh." She sent a silent prayer heavenward then approached the driver's side of her car.

"Got a spare?"

Rather than nervousness, hummingbird wings took flight at the sound of Constable Jack's voice as she met his gaze.

"Here, I'll take a look." He offered her his oversize umbrella.

She held it over her head and shuddered as a chill tore through her. *Of all the days to venture to the market.*

As Jack fetched the spare tire tucked into a compartment in the hatchback, she vowed to better prepare for the High Country climate. Near Phoenix where she'd lived previously, the temperatures range between triple digits, and being cool and dry. Except for monsoon season, which was a weather condition that occurred in Sweetwater, as well.

"Looks like you need a new spare, Doc. But this one should get you to Hank and Gordie's."

The constable's words interrupted her thoughts about the weather, and she watched as he pulled a jack from the same compartment.

While he hitched up the back end of the SUV, she stifled a huff. A bystander would certainly consider her reaction unreasonable in light of Jack's help. But at the same time, his take-charge boldness hit too close to her ex-husband's controlling nature. Not once during their marriage had Aaron treated her as an equal partner.

That's when it clicked.

Spagnoletti.

The brother of Aaron's mother was named Harold Spagnoletti. And before her ex-husband's career had imploded due to his fraudulent business dealings, he'd served as a partner with a major development company.

In all innocence, Emerson had overheard a conversation about a lucrative trade deal in the works. Located in a small, Northern Arizona town.

She was going to be sick.

Chapter Six

Jack was lying flat on his back beneath Emerson's car, the late-fall rain now subsiding to a trickle. Earlier, when he'd spotted her car as he drove past the community college, a nudge to his spirit had prodded him to swerve into the lot. And as soon as he spied the flat tire on the SUV, he'd chalked up the detour as a divine appointment.

His original destination had been the preschool to surprise Josie with a bit of father-daughter time before the evening's scheduled surveillance. And ever since the vet had showed up on his doorstep, he couldn't seem to be around her enough.

All in the name of business. As if the more he repeated that thought, the more he might start to believe it. Except that the stakeouts were turning out to be a complete bust.

Regardless, he enjoyed hearing Josie regale him with stories—her sweet lisp music to his ears— about her visits to the preserve with Miss Lacey after preschool. And their evenings bundled up in blankets on the patio lounge chairs, the "place" heaters full-blast below a canopy of stars. But under the surface, guilt still rankled, since the majority of his time had been committed to his job both on and off the clock.

It was those murmurs across the cell connection, though, Emerson's husky undertones—and one night in particular—that continued to melt his defenses.

Errant flakes had twinkled in the security lights as they'd swirled through the air. Stepping from the shadows, he'd snagged a glimpse of Emerson in a clearing, silvery flecks catching in her hair as she twirled. It had mesmerized him. And then she'd startled, the whites of her eyes flashing as he'd stepped into view.

"You weren't supposed to see that." She recovered, giggling nervously as she spread her arms wide. "This reminds me of when I was Josie's age." Dark eyes shining, her full lips had lifted in a wistful smile. "And my mom and dad took me to the mountains where I experienced my first snowfall."

Jack's own Christmases had been tainted ever since the year his father had left home. One of the many reasons he worked hard to create idyllic memories for Josie.

Dressed in a sweatshirt and jeans, Emerson had shivered as she rubbed her hands the length of her arms. "And then a few years later, my mom was killed by a drunk driver."

It was that piece of her story that broke Jack's heart for the little girl she once was. Yet despite his growing feelings for her, her overreaction in his living area—fright etched into the delicate skin around her wide, mocha-colored eyes, and her revulsion to Jack's gun-handling inquiry—kept him from testing her boundaries.

Her footfalls silent, then, she'd approached him as they wrapped up surveillance and reached out. Her featherlight touch against his light jacket a reminder that rather than wear his feelings on his sleeve, he'd pinned them to his collar.

And before they'd parted ways that night, he'd wondered what it would take for them both to reveal their hidden hurts.

The hard, cold ground drove Jack from his wandering thoughts.

"Say, can you hand me that wrench in the tool bag?"

A minute ticked by with no response. Shimmying against the pavement from beneath the belly of the two-ton vehicle, errant drops spritzed the air. But there was no sign of Emerson.

The campus parking lot had thinned out since he'd started changing the flat, which was taking longer than he'd anticipated. *These newer cars.*

Shaking his head, he caught sight of Emerson with her back to him where she was hunched over beside a maple, its seasonally vibrant purple leaves faded and strewn across the grassy area.

He splashed through the standing water, grateful for the boots he wore…and for remembering to dress Josie that morning in her polka-dot galoshes.

"Hey, you okay?" It looked as if he'd once again

interrupted her in the midst of a vulnerable situation.

Wiping her mouth with the back of her hand, Emerson straightened to reveal the ashen shade that had replaced her olive tone.

"I'll be okay." But her demeanor said otherwise.

"Get in the car and dry out. I'll drive you back to the clinic and have Hank or Gordie pick up your car."

Narrowed eyes and bunched shoulders transformed Emerson's appearance, not unlike a cat ready to pounce.

Preparing himself for an argument, he held up his hands as he quickly backtracked. "Or whatever you want—just say the word."

He watched as the fight swept through Emerson in tandem with the rivulets traversing the parking lot gutters. In that moment, Jack wanted nothing more than to make life easier for her. To brush the glittery drops of moisture from her thick lashes and to safeguard her from the memories that triggered her defensiveness.

Even if he was unwilling to open himself up to invite a relationship, he was able to offer friendship. In the same way he would to any one of the Sweetwater townsfolk.

Because that's what he did. *Serve and protect.*

Except when it came to Willow. But as he faced Emerson, it was as if his past confronted him in that space, and he realized Persh had been right.

There'd been no signs of illness for him to miss; and that nothing in his power could have changed the outcome.

He sucked in a sharp breath, dizzy with awareness.

"Thank you."

Barely discernible, Emerson's voice broke into his thoughts. There was a subtle change in her protective posture, one that drifted between resignation and an unnamed emotion. Could it be gratitude?

"Just doing my duty, ma'am," he drawled, then tipped his Stetson, causing water to drip from the hat's brim and a twinkle to brighten Emerson's eyes.

And before he could put a lid on it, a longing to know how he could see more of that sparkle washed over him in the same fashion as the earlier downfall.

"I'll just tell Carley to expect me at the clinic on the later side."

While she ducked into the driver's seat of her SUV and contacted the preserve, he considered his options. Given Emerson's preference for taking matters into her own hands, he'd ask if she'd be okay accompanying him to the preschool. Even though the window of opportunity had passed to pick up Josie early, his little girl would want to spend time with the pup when they returned Emerson to the clinic.

Not only had the dog captured Josie's heart, but the child also treasured her visits with "Mith Em" and getting to see Petey and Buzzy, and Alvin and Louie.

A knock on the window rattled him. Emerson beckoned him with her finger to hop in the passenger's seat. Although the rain had let up, dampness clung to his skin. He imagined Emerson must be freezing in the lightweight jacket she wore.

After sliding onto the bucket seat next to her, he pulled the door shut. The intimacy within the enclosed space caught him off guard, his throat hitching. Yet he wasn't opposed to it, a faint hint of lavender suspended in the cramped quarters. Did Emerson sense it, too?

"I asked Carley to call the tow. So if you could drop me off at the clinic…"

Emerson smiled, the glimmer of hope in her eyes unmistakable.

"You took the words right out of my mouth."

The sigh of relief that slipped between her lips was all the thanks he needed. "Would it be all right with you if we stopped at the preschool to pick up Josie on the way?" Given the connection between the veterinarian and his daughter, he didn't think she would object to the detour.

Yet one of the simple reasons he avoided the topic of dating was his refusal to involve Josie in a relationship that might not last for the long haul. Inviting Emerson into their lives any more than the status quo could easily be a huge risk. But was it one he was ready to take?

"Sounds perfect." Emerson hesitated before they exited her vehicle, the crease between her eyebrows deepening. "Do I just leave my keys in the car?"

He chuckled. "I know that's not how it works in the city. But no need to worry here." *Except for the vandalism at the preserve.* Which still baffled him.

After Emerson had stowed her keys, he opened the cruiser's passenger door for her then hopped behind the wheel before buckling up. After adjusting the heat to full blast and shifting into Drive, Jack whispered a quick prayer they would catch the culprits soon. Time was running out.

The town council would not allow the nonprofit to run indefinitely. And he wasn't prepared to tack on one more thing to his litany of failures. Even those concerns that were out of his control.

"Are we still on for tonight?" Emerson's eyes remained fixed on the road in front of them.

During the most recent stakeouts, their routine had been to set up in a new spot before circling the perimeter and then meeting at an agreed-upon area to view both the entrance and exits. But he'd begun to think their approach might've been all wrong. Because the more he considered it, the more it appeared to be an inside job.

He was tempted to burst out laughing if the

situation had been at all humorous. Because that would mean pointing fingers at a mangy slew of rescues as the culprits.

Instead, that left them back at square one. *Who was behind the damage, and why?*

All he knew was that something had to give, and soon.

The question was: would it be the underlying tension between him and his dark-haired partner who harbored a passel of secrets? Or would it be a break in the case?

Clearing her throat, Emerson tapped him on the shoulder, his skin heating at her touch.

"Um, earth to Jack?"

He jerked his head in her direction, where she gazed at him with a curious expression.

He scratched the stubble on his chin. "Sorry, I was, uh, just contemplating how we might change things up."

"Or maybe you should spend the evening with Josie." Her teeth chattering, she clutched her jacket tighter.

The clouds had since parted, with the remaining leaves clinging to trees heavy with moisture. Even with the car heater chugging away, their damp clothing couldn't dry fast enough. His notion to convene in a different area that afforded less protection from the elements was only asking for trouble.

"I may take you up on that offer." He didn't attempt to mask the disappointment in his tone as he parked the cruiser.

Facing her again in the seat next to him, she seemed smaller and more vulnerable. And although he desired to solve this spree of vandalism, it would mean less intentional time with Emerson. But he could use a free evening to regroup.

"Want to come in or wait in the car?" Over the past few weeks, he'd come to sense how important it was for her to make her own decisions without his interference.

"I'll come in, thanks." She unbuckled her seat belt. "When Lacey brought Josie to the preserve the last time, she mentioned Sunday church service and I wanted to take a quick peek inside."

"Sure thing." During their surveillance stints, he'd also learned they shared the same faith, which reassured him she was not alone in her struggles.

He pushed open the door to the preschool, where they saw Miss Marie clacking away at the keyboard in front of her. "What a surprise!" She smoothed her simple dress as she rose from her chair.

"Hi, Miss Marie, this is Emerson, er... Dr. Parker from the preserve and sanctuary." He coughed, then clasped Emerson's fingers to draw her closer. The contact sent a zing up his arm and his gaze snapped to hers. But her expression remained neutral.

"Oh, I've already had the pleasure of meeting the doc at the B and B."

Emerson's hand slipped from his as Marie enveloped her in a welcoming embrace.

"It's so good to see you again, Emerson."

"You, too, Miss Marie."

A slight tremor in her voice belied her outward calm, causing a sudden case of cat-got-his-tongue to render Jack silent.

A nervous chuckle escaped Emerson's lips.

Coughing, he tugged on his collar. "I thought I'd surprise Josie and pick her up a bit early, but…"

Marie clapped her hands together, oblivious to the silent interaction between him and the doc. "Oh, she'll be delighted to see you anyway. Let me call her teacher."

While Marie dialed into Josie's classroom with the same efficiency with which she'd run the B and B following the passing of Lacey's Gram, he rocked back on his heels. The weight of Emerson's gaze drilled into him. He turned to find her staring, eyebrows arched and brown eyes shifting back and forth between him and the part-time secretary. And then she winked.

What was running through Emerson's mind? Jaw unhinged, he returned his attention to Miss Marie, whose keen observation pinned them both from beneath her lashes.

Was the veterinarian teasing him?

Just then, his pint-size girl barreled into his legs, arms encircling his knees. "Daddy!"

He pretended to wobble, which induced one of her famous giggles, before he hoisted her against his chest.

"Mith Em!" Josie waved her neon-pink backpack at Emerson, who appeared to be holding up the wall in the corner of the small office. His mother had accused him of doing that very same thing as a young boy—the weight of his father's desertion resting on his then-bony shoulders.

"Thank you, Miss Marie. See you in church."

"My pleasure, Constable. And it's always a treat, Emerson." The woman smiled warmly, her hazel eyes assessing.

Emerson waggled her fingers. "Say 'hi' to Lacey for me."

The three of them made their way down the short flight of stairs before Jack snapped his fingers. "Oh! You mentioned taking a look at the sanctuary?"

A few feet ahead of him and Josie, Emerson's braid swung against her back like a pendulum. Spinning toward him, as he took in the sight of her flushed cheeks, full lips and bright almond-shaped eyes, his heart stilled a beat. While he'd always considered Emerson attractive, at this moment it was as if he was seeing her through different eyes. Eyes that had remained true to Willow until her passing.

Yet this new catch in his heart indicated a shift between the two of them. Could she, too, sense their developing closeness?

Oblivious to his inner turmoil, she smiled.

"I'll wait until Sunday. Maybe Miss Marie can show me around."

There it was again. That teasing lilt lacing her tone.

And then she sashayed toward the passenger side of the cruiser. *Sashayed!*

He would miss that evening's stakeout, of that he had no doubt. Eventually he would need to address the dynamics that transpired between them. But right now he needed to formulate a new plan and get to the bottom of the shenanigans.

And a call to Persh was at the top of his list.

"And then I visited Huey, Louie and…"

On this Sunday morning that had dawned with blue skies, Jack listened as Josie ticked off the animals she'd visited during her latest trip to the preserve with Lacey.

When he'd brought Emerson back to her apartment earlier in the week, Josie had given pets to the rescue pup and then father and daughter had spent a fair amount of quality time together—a much-needed reprieve for them both. Then he'd called the town councilman to get his take on the vandalism.

He'd also mentioned his suspicions that it could

be an inside job. And as a stab of remorse sliced through him, he'd questioned Persh on whether the hiring committee had conducted a background check on Emerson. At the time, he'd justified his interest by wanting to understand the woman better. But even with the vandalism beginning shortly before her arrival, it was hard to chalk it up as co-incidence when it had only escalated.

"And then Mith Em let me play with Dewey!"

Josie's singsong voice snagged his attention. "Dewey?" That wasn't a familiar name.

"Thilly Daddy, the dog we found!"

He snapped his fingers. "Of course!"

Nosing into the church parking lot, he scanned the cars for a certain white SUV.

He'd checked in with Hank Valentine, who ran the full-service garage in town. The mechanic had confirmed that he'd towed Emerson's vehicle, replaced its tire and returned her car to the preserve all on the same day. One of the many benefits of small-town living.

He retrieved Josie from the back seat, then the pair headed across the pavement. He looked forward to worshipping with the folks at Sweetwater Community Church, where he could clear his mind of all things vandalism, town council and lack of funds.

But as soon as he and Josie entered through the double doors, his tongue felt like sandpaper as his focus shifted to Emerson—a stunning vision in a flattering purple sweater dress paired with denim leggings and black, knee-high boots. She wore her hair loose, the rich mahogany tresses framing her exotic face. Not wishing to interrupt her conversation with the town's baker, and also afraid standing there with his mouth hanging open, he bypassed the two women before sidling into another aisle toward the rear of the sanctuary.

"Daddy."

Josie whispered in his ear and he chuckled at her futile attempt to master the art. He gave her his full attention.

"I want to thit by Mith Em."

She pointed to where Annie had directed Emerson—to a row of seats near the front of the room. And although he still wrestled with residual guilt surrounding his late wife, sweet memories that he attributed to Emerson's presence replaced the sad ones with each passing day.

By the time he and Josie maneuvered up the aisle, due to several interruptions by the townsfolk, only two empty seats remained and they were located right next to Emerson. She met his eyes, her dark eyebrows quirked.

"Are these chairs available?" Nodding at the spots, with his free hand he tugged at the tie he blamed for constricting the flow of blood to his brain.

Emerson's face brightened with a smile that warmed him from his dress Stetson to his shiny cowboy boots. Now all he needed was Pastor Mark to deliver a riveting sermon. Otherwise, he doubted his ability to concentrate on much of anything sitting shoulder-to-shoulder with the veterinarian.

"They aren't anymore." She winked, snatching the bulletin from one of the cushioned seats.

Settling Josie between the two of them, he figured the extra space would help him to rein in his erratic pulse. He busied himself by pulling a box of crayons from his daughter's "Miss Lacey bag" in case she stayed for the service rather than attend children's church.

"Hi, Mith Em." Josie placed her hand atop Emerson's.

"Hello, Miss Josie." The doc intertwined her fingers with his child's as if it was the most natural response in the world.

As he witnessed a host of emotions flit across Emerson's smooth skin, a shadow clouded her eyes, triggering a pang of shame that had to do with the request he'd made of Persh. But he'd already decided that as soon as he met up with his friend, he'd call off the background check. He wanted to hear her story if—and only if—she was ready to share it with him.

With that matter resolved, he settled into his seat to join in worship with the congregation. Scanning the sanctuary, he located Annie seated next to former volunteer firefighter Josh Rogers.

As so happened, the town council had been able to garner enough funds to hire the fire department's single full-time, salaried employee. While he was happy for Josh, the young man's promotion only served to highlight Jack's losing battle on the precinct side.

Josh lowered his head toward Annie, and something he said caused a pink flush to spread across the baker's cheeks before she swatted the burly firefighter's arm with her church bulletin. Stifling a chuckle with the back of his hand, Jack recalled Josh telling him about his unsuccessful attempts to convince Annie to date a man in uniform.

Perhaps that was a job for the Sweetwater legend. He snorted just as Pastor Mark welcomed members and visitors, before diving into his sermon based on the Book of Solomon and the blessing of companionship, as well as the rewards of people who worked together.

He snuck a peek at Emerson. The woman had appeared in his life at the height of his most challenging and busiest season. As if commissioned by the good Lord, Himself to share Jack's burdens.

Just then the pager in his pocket went off. One glimpse and his heart sank. Because not only was an uninterrupted service impossible, but he also needed Emerson's help. Again.

Inclining his head toward her, the scent of lavender triggered an instant calm. "I need to head into the station." He spoke low to avoid disrupting the other parishioners.

"Go."

When she placed her slim hand on his forearm, the familiar zing traveled across his nerve endings.

"I'll call you." He kissed Josie atop her head, then brushed past Emerson, ignoring the gentle tug on his heart to stay.

Pacing the closet-size cubicle that served as his office, he pinned Councilman Persh to his spot. "Are you sure?" At this point, the question was unnecessary, as his buddy had already confirmed the evidence.

"I don't want to believe it, either." Persh was seated on one of two folding chairs in the corner of the makeshift room, a Styrofoam cup of day-old coffee perched on his lap.

He restated the news he'd shared upon Jack's arrival, which had explained his absence at church.

"Someone tipped off the town council. An emergency meeting was convened. That's everything I know."

Standing stock-still, he scratched the nape of his neck, where his hair grew unruly. "If it's true that someone is pilfering money from the preserve's petty cash, that could prove the vandalism is an inside job." Fixing his gaze on Persh, he begged him to disagree. Because if that was the case, it only added to his suspicions surrounding Emerson. And he didn't want to go there. Yet this had been the first time money had been involved. *Allegedly.*

"Oh, about that background check on Doc Parker..." Persh tossed the cup in the overflowing trash can.

Jack's hand shot up. "I retract my request—it was out of line."

The councilman leveled a look at him, his gaze discerning. "At the very least, I'd recommend setting up temporary cameras on the preserve."

Jack frowned. "Got a camera plant growing in your garden?"

"Very funny." Persh unfolded his legs. "I'll loan some extra equipment from the B and B."

The two of them worked out the details, and a couple of hours later he finally rolled onto the preserve grounds. It wouldn't surprise him if the escalating safety concerns drove the tourists and townsfolk away. His promise to his late wife rang in his ears, dogging his steps.

But as soon as he strode into the clinic, his heart softened as Josie skipped over to him. A happy and healthy Dewey was running circles around his daughter, tail wagging and tongue lolling. Emerson emerged from an exam room, a docile chicken in her arms. Any uncertainties he'd dared consider about her involvement in the latest development dissipated.

And it was then he admitted how easy it would

be to fall in love with her. But at his very core, he feared his ability to keep Emerson safe, and that he would lose her, too.

Yet the hunger in his heart for what he desired—what he didn't feel he deserved—only intensified as he swung his gaze toward her, his breath nearly raked from his lungs. He palmed the back of his neck in an attempt to get a grip.

"Well, look what the cat dragged in." Emerson laughed, patting the chicken on its downy head.

If she sensed his unease, she didn't let on.

"Where?" Josie grasped the colorful ball she'd been tossing to Dewey and twirled in place.

Emerson giggled, causing his stomach to drop to his knees.

"Just something silly that grown-ups say." Handing the chicken to a volunteer, she beckoned him toward his daughter and the golden retriever, who looked like a completely different pooch thanks to Emerson's healing touch. He still believed Dewey would be good for Emerson to keep with her as a companion on the grounds.

"Your daughter is quite attached."

"I think he's right where he's supposed to be." Tamping down his feelings for the time being, he shifted his stance. "Say, could I ask a favor?"

"Of course."

He'd nosed a booted foot against the floor, his hands tucked into his pockets. He was a man unaccustomed to asking for help, and Emerson had already brought his daughter back to the clinic following the church service.

"What's up?" Her face revealed an openness that invited him to continue.

"Would you mind driving Josie home while Persh and I install some cameras?" He held his breath as Emerson's mouth formed an O.

"I'd be honored to." And then she smirked. "And no extra charge for a bedtime story."

The woman had no clue as to the emotions she drummed up, thoughts of her tucking Josie into bed conjuring images he felt unworthy to entertain. But he'd handed her his extra key and she left with his child as soon as Persh showed up. The two of them made quick work of installing a handful of cameras strategically located throughout the grounds.

Although there was no way to be certain what—if anything—would come of it, he prayed for a breakthrough.

He only hoped it wouldn't point to the good doctor. Because not only had he placed his trust in her with the care of his child, but he'd also begun to entrust her with his fragile heart.

As he headed home, a breeze kicked up. With Thanksgiving only a week away, the colder weather was a sure sign that winter was close behind. Returning home, he found Emerson curled up on his sofa, her stocking feet curled beneath her.

When she didn't immediately acknowledge his presence, he took the opportunity to admire her striking beauty, acknowledging to himself how she fit seamlessly into his family. The sudden realization took him by surprise and he bit back a growl.

Emerson startled, her spine straightening. But when her gaze landed on him, she sunk back against the cushions. Setting a magazine on the coffee table, the unguarded smile she offered unsettled him.

It would be so easy to give in to his feelings. But the town's constable was running scared.

Struggling to maintain an arm's length distance, he thanked her for the help with a promise to be in touch.

And as he watched her beguiling smile slip from her lips, disappointment clouded her eyes and his stomach clenched at his cowardice.

Three days later, he pressed his mobile phone against his ear and Persh's voice bloomed across the connection loud and clear.

"The cameras picked up something."

Chapter Seven

It was a delightfully mild autumn day in Sweetwater. After living the majority of her life in a suburb near Phoenix—which experienced little deviation in the weather throughout the year—Emerson relished the cooler temperatures in the pine tree-dotted mountains. And even though she'd been forewarned by Annie and Lacey to expect snow any day, she anticipated the four seasons in the High Country with the excitement of a child.

"So what's happening with you and the constable?" Annie asked, observing Emerson as a mama bird watched over her hatchlings.

She couldn't hold back the infinitesimal tilt of her lips at the mention of the man who'd slipped through her defenses, right alongside his adorable pigtailed daughter.

"Aha, I knew it!" Lacey's russet-colored curls bounced in time with her stride as she pushed through the swinging door into the inn's dining area. The three women basked in the sun's afternoon rays that shone through the picture window, minute dust particles dancing in the air.

Because it was a slower day midweek at the preserve, she'd decided to play catch-up with her new friends and to discuss the upcoming Thanksgiving meal, as well as brainstorm ideas for the annual Christmas boutique.

Her stomach ached from laughing alongside these ladies, with Lacey's exuberance triggering another round of giggles as the woman poured generous servings of iced sweet water into tumblers for her and Annie.

"I'm sorry to disappoint you ladies, but the stakeouts at the preserve are the only things happening."

She didn't miss Annie's glance at Lacey, her eyebrows waggling as she adopted a singsong tone much like that of Jack's daughter. "That's not what I heard."

Lacey jumped right in to pick up the thread of conversation. "And I hear you're no stranger to the constable's cottage." Covering her mouth with her free hand, she hid an exaggerated mock-expression of shock.

Emerson glanced at one woman and then the other, round eyes aghast. "And here I thought gossip was frowned upon."

All three women burst into another fit of laughter as Persh came strolling through the swinging door, a cookie dangling from his lips and crumbs stuck to his goatee.

"Drew Pershing!" Lacey eyed her husband's stash.

He swallowed the sugary treat in one bite.

"What's got you ladies cackling in here like hens?"

The heat rose to Emerson's face. "My new friends are making up stories!" Feigning surprise, she pointed an accusing finger at Lacey and Annie in turn.

"Don't let them scare you away, Doc." Persh winked, siding with her. "Say, the constable is looking for you."

Shooting up against the high-back chair, she hitched a thumb at herself. "Me?"

Lacey and Annie exchanged knowing glances.

Persh nodded. "Maybe give him a call when you're free."

She automatically assumed Jack needed her to babysit Josie again. And she certainly wouldn't give the request a second thought. Spending time with the little girl brightened her week, right next to surveillance duty. She remembered the rainy afternoon, then, when Jack had shown up to rescue her. And she'd subsequently rejected his chivalry, stiffening at his attempt to take charge. From years of powerlessness, that independent streak of hers had morphed into defensiveness.

While it would have been the ideal opportunity to open up to Jack, he'd surprised her by giving her the option of how she preferred to handle her flat tire. Right after she'd realized her ex-husband had been the perpetrator behind the developer scandal.

"You'll be coming to dinner, then?" Lacey broke the silence, Persh having vacated the dining area.

Emerson sensed the weight of both women's stares. "Sorry, what was that?"

Lacey's green eyes twinkled with mirth as she glanced at Annie. "Just like I thought."

Winking, Lacey faced her again. "I'm taking head count for Thanksgiving and I told Persh I didn't want to hear no for an answer."

The ladies could think what they wanted about her and Jack. But now her curiosity was piqued as to why the constable wanted to speak with her.

"Only if I can bring something." Swallowing the last sip of iced water from the pine-tree-etched glassware, she savored the sweet aftertaste as she dabbed her mouth with a cloth napkin.

"Let me figure out the menu and I'll reach out." Lacey began collecting the soiled dishes. "I hate to shoo you both, but I need to prepare for a few new overnight guests."

Accepting hugs from her two friends, Emerson skipped down the steps along the pavement toward the guest parking area. With no appointments on the afternoon schedule at the clinic, rather than call Jack, as Persh suggested, she opted to take a drive and enjoy the gorgeous afternoon.

The balmy weekend weather generated more tourists, so the commute was a bit slower as she steered her SUV along the familiar route toward

Main Street. If the constable's cruiser was parked in its customary spot outside his cottage, she'd drop by to find out what he wanted. And, hopefully, get to be on the receiving end of Miss Josie's hugs.

As she navigated through the stoplights and four-way intersections, she finished replaying the exchange in the campus parking lot, followed by the detour to the preschool. Even though she'd teased Jack about the older woman, it had been a ploy to mask her response to the feel of Jack's rough fingers looping around hers.

Which had then sparked a twinge of envy at the idea of Jack dating another woman. He may still be nursing wounds over his loss, but that hadn't stopped a shift between them, a softening of sorts.

Or maybe she's simply been serving as a means to an end in his life—both with the stakeouts, and the extra assistance with Josie.

Rolling down the street, the cruiser came into view, along with a vacant spot in front of the picturesque historic home. She quickly located Jack and Josie outdoors, where the constable's daughter was coloring on the sidewalk with broken pieces of chalk. Jack picked weeds that poked through the front lawn, which was sprinkled with errant leaves that had dropped from the blaze maples lining the boulevard.

Before she'd even planted her two feet on the

ground, Josie was running toward her as fast as her little legs could carry her.

Tossing her arms around Emerson's knees, the child clung on as if for dear life. "Mith Em!"

"Oomph!" Pretending to lose her balance, she teetered on her heeled boots. This launched Josie into giggles, not unlike those the three women had shared that afternoon.

Jack pushed up from his position where he crouched on the grass. "Hey, stranger."

He approached her, a neutral expression on his whiskered face. Although devoid of clues, she didn't miss his appreciative gaze, which elicited the same flush that had crept over her skin when teased by her girlfriends.

And from her vantage point, he wasn't faring much better if the hard yank of his flannel shirt and clearing of his throat meant anything.

"So…you just happened to be in the neighborhood?"

Bolstered by the possibility that she wasn't the only one battling feelings yet undefined, she licked her parched lips. "Persh said you were looking for me?"

Comprehension registered in his eyes and he nodded. "Oh. Right!"

"Daddy?" Josie released Emerson's legs and gazed up at her father, eyes brimming with adoration.

The near-tangible love between father and

daughter washed over Emerson, her heart swelling in that familiar way.

Without hesitating, Jack lifted Josie into his arms so they were at eye level. "What's up, Jose?"

The little girl leaned her head closer to Jack's to stage-whisper in his ear.

"Can Mith Em help with the poppy corn?"

Emerson heard the exchange, attempting to stifle her smile.

Jack's piercing eyes captured her attention over the top of his daughter's fair hair. He deposited Josie on the sidewalk at his booted feet. "Why don't you ask Miss Em if she'd care to stay?"

She didn't need to be asked twice, but waited with patience for Josie to approach her. Squatting down to the child's level, she peeked at Jack through her lashes. She couldn't begin to imagine what he was thinking. Was it police business stealing through his mind? Or something more?

And that something more had been near the top of her prayer requests since her first and subsequent run-ins with the constable. Petitions for a clear sign if—and when—the time was right to open her heart to love again.

"Mith Em, Daddy and I want you to thtay and help us with poppy corn."

With a tender touch, Josie patted her cheek. Her lids fluttered closed and her heart squeezed as she savored the sensation.

"Okay?"

Her lids popped open to meet Josie's hopeful gaze. Slipping her fingers between the child's, she stood. "I'd be honored." And as Josie skipped beside her toward the cozy cottage, with Jack trailing behind, Emerson beamed from the inside out.

Not that she'd expected anything to have changed since her last time at Jack's home when she'd read his daughter a bedtime story and tucked her in, but once inside, she stopped short at the absence of several photos.

A lightness swept through her. Could that be some kind of sign?

Jack stepped around her to help Josie wash her hands at the kitchen sink. Emerson shook her head. *It was too late.* Because sign or no sign, she'd already opened her heart to father and daughter.

But was Jack ready to open his?

The remainder of the afternoon coasted into evening as the three of them sat around the kitchen table, with Josie kneeling on a chair between the adults. Conversation flowed, mostly about town news and what to expect at the Pershings's annual Thanksgiving gathering.

With child-safe, oversize plastic needles and floss, they strung fresh popcorn—sans the kernels that Jack had burned—next to plump, ruby-red cranberries. Amidst plenty of opportunities to nibble on dropped pieces of fruit and the salty snack, and ample giggles when caught in the act.

A soy candle that Jack lit burned its pumpkin scent, adding a touch of hominess and tranquility to the waning day. Emerson couldn't recall engaging in anything during her marriage resembling that afternoon's activity. Why Aaron married her to begin with, she would never understand. Because as hard as she tried, she'd been unable to live up to his expectations. But here, with Jack and Josie—and among her new friends Lacey, Persh and Annie—she experienced what she could only describe as acceptance. A prayer of thanks stirred in her heart.

Within seconds, however, the warmth was replaced by a sick feeling in her stomach. How would Jack react if he learned that her ex-husband had been involved in the scandal and previous vandalism? Would he hold it against her?

She had been clueless about Aaron's business dealings, which he'd always kept from her with the excuse that it would distract her from her job at the clinic, and her role as his wife. Making it easy to turn a blind eye to the secrets he hid from her.

If only she'd been stronger at the time. She sniffled as an image of her Aunt Francine stole through her mind. Although she missed the woman with a deep ache, she was grateful her aunt had been spared the shambles of her niece's life.

"Hey...you okay?"

Jack's outdoorsy aftershave, mingling with

a trace of pumpkin that lingered after the wick burned down, tickled her nose as he leaned close. Pulse shifting into overdrive, she was certain he could hear the steady thud.

Swallowing hard, she remained perfectly still. Because turning her head—even a smidgen— would bring their lips together.

She couldn't remember the last time she'd kissed another man other than her ex-husband. Even then, intimacies had been rare. *But it had only taken once.*

"I'm done!" Brandishing the empty bowl littered with popcorn remnants, Josie's gap-toothed grin revealed lips stained with berry juice.

Saved by a five-year-old. She exhaled as they refocused their attention on the child sandwiched in the middle of their trio.

Which allowed additional time to process what was between her and the constable.

But she had a feeling that it was already too late to reclaim her heart.

Chapter Eight

Jack still buzzed each time he pictured the three of them stringing popcorn in the homey confines of his kitchen, the scented candle he'd dug out from a shelf in the back of his closet adding to the coziness.

But it was the depth of pain that pooled in Emerson's eyes after he'd inquired about her well-being that weighed heavily on his heart. Of course, his own fight-or-flight response had threatened to kick in early on—he'd wavered between escorting her out to her car with a random excuse, and exploring what neither of them had yet been willing to confront.

Or maybe he was completely off base and his thoughts were the result of an overactive imagination.

Yet, the pulse trembling against her slender neck when their eyes locked conveyed to him they were on the same page.

But were they reading from the same book?

By the time he'd settled Josie into her princess bed—with promises to string the backyard foliage with the garland they'd made—he'd returned to the kitchen to find Emerson clearing the supplies from their activity and putting away the slices of pizza leftover from the delivery order.

She'd stifled her yawns, a clear signal that it wasn't the right time to discuss their potential feelings toward each other, or the evidence Persh had discovered on the surveillance videos a couple days earlier.

Now, propped on the edge of a bistro chair in the preserve's live-in quarters, the rhythmic pumping of his booted foot belied his customarily calm exterior.

"I'm just putting on my earrings." Emerson's voice carried from behind an ornate, hand-painted antique-rattan room screen erected in the corner of the small space.

Tonight was the night.

He, Josie and Emerson had been invited to join the Pershings for the evening—along with several other friends—for a traditional Thanksgiving meal with all the trimmings. Lacey had started the annual gathering not long after she'd permanently returned to Sweetwater, with the attendance ebbing and flowing each year.

But over the last few years, the event had become a high point, and also a special way to give Josie the experience of a family tradition.

And because Emerson was the newest resident in town, he felt it only right to offer her a lift to the B and B. Yet, if he was one-hundred-percent honest, it served as a safe way for him to test the waters. A first date, of sorts.

Earlier that afternoon, he'd dropped off Josie at the inn to give him a few hours at the station to play catchup on the stacks of administrative paperwork. And then, before long, it had been time to get ready for the party of the year.

One laced with anticipation, and an underlying intimacy, compared to recent Thanksgivings past. No doubt due to a particular veterinarian he couldn't stop thinking about.

The one thing he could be certain of was that the Pershings would pull out all the stops to create an equally delightful and memorable occasion for everyone in attendance.

"Take your time." Willing his leg to stop jittering, he removed his Stetson and worked it between his hands.

When he'd arrived a few minutes earlier, he'd let himself in as she finished accessorizing her outfit. Now he yanked on the bolo tie looped around his starched collar, his nerves getting the best of him.

"I need a favor."

He stiffened at the sound of her throaty voice. But when she emerged from behind the screen, his breath hitched at the sight of her. Fingers loosening their grip, his hat tumbled to the floor at his feet.

Rather than the signature plait that hung down

her back and swayed with each step as she walked, her thick dark hair tumbled freely over her shoulders. A black sheath in a gauzy fabric grazed her knees, capped sleeves highlighting her toned arms.

He swallowed the ever-present lump in his throat while in her presence, his Stetson all but forgotten atop his dress boots.

He coughed into his hand, eyeing the room. "You still got furniture to move?"

Emerson laughed, a musical melody he didn't think he'd ever tire of.

Her glossy lips shimmered, and suddenly he pitied the awkward schoolboys with insufferable crushes on the cute girls in class.

"Not this time." Emerson winked, her fringe of lashes framing mocha-colored eyes that appeared larger than life. Spinning in place, she pointed to the area just below her hairline and thrust out her palm. "But would you please fasten this chain?"

Was it his mind playing tricks on him, or had her voice grown huskier?

As Emerson lifted the thick curls off her back, his eyes traced the creamy expanse of her exposed neck. Sucking in a lungful of the cloying air, the unconscious act of breathing became difficult.

"Uh…sure." After grabbing his hat from the floor, he pushed it down onto his head, relieved he'd been able to squeeze in a much-needed trim for the evening's gala. From the number of barbershop clientele he'd tallied while sitting in the chair, every other male who called Sweetwater home picked up on the same idea.

Now he stood behind Emerson, the prospect of melting and leaving a puddle at her feet more likely by the second. Heat radiated from her nearness, his lids drifting closed as he inhaled the lavender fragrance that conjured colorful meadows, sunshine and hope. The very same things she'd brought into both his and Josie's lives without even knowing it.

While divine timing had proven best on numerous occasions in the past, he could only guess at Emerson's plans. Could she be ready to embrace him and his daughter, alongside a life dedicated to caring for the winged and four-legged rescues within the Sweetwater community?

"Constable?"

Emerson craned her elegant neck, no doubt in an attempt to see what held him up.

"Sorry." He mumbled something unintelligible under his breath, his hands shaking. At the rate he was going, there was no way he'd be able to connect the delicate chain he'd plucked from her outstretched hand.

Biting his lower lip in apt concentration, he steadied his fingers and the catch finally fastened.

"Whew!" Just when he'd assumed he was in the clear, his hand slipped and grazed her skin. He flinched as if burned, while Emerson appeared oblivious to his struggles.

As she dropped her hands to her sides, the waves spilled over her shoulders and he resisted the urge to fan himself with his hat.

Pivoting in his direction, her dazzling grin charged his insides like static electricity during one of their lightning storms.

"Thank you so much—sorry to keep you waiting."

Glancing around her apartment, Emerson's gaze latched onto a pair of black velvet slingbacks. She padded across the room and stepped into them, which accentuated her long and shapely legs. Grabbing a matching clutch with a strap draped across a bistro chair, she faced him.

"Ready?" Expectation colored her tone.

As a father, Jack could appreciate the ancient saying that referred to being putty in someone's hands. But as the woman next to him removed a wool coat and scarf from the wooden rack near the door, he compared that concept to the Bible story about a potter and the clay. He only hoped Emerson had the ability to see beyond the oftentimes messy work in progress as he strived to be a better man. A man who might one day be worthy of her affection.

"Oh, I almost forgot!" She snapped her fingers before retrieving a glass container from the refrigerator.

A few minutes later, they were settled on the front seat of Jack's vehicle. The traffic was sparse as they cruised toward the inn. And as they passed through an intersection, the sky blossomed into a dazzling sunset streaked with pinks, oranges and violets.

"Wow," Emerson said, her tone awestruck.

Jack peeked sideways before returning his eyes to the road. A burnished lock hid her profile. Although he still hadn't divulged what he'd learned about the surveillance-cam detail, he needed to tell her soon so she'd have a better idea of what to look for during her shifts.

Because there'd been no mistaking that the college student sporting the black pixie cut had dipped into the box of petty cash a handful of times. They were still waiting for her to come into the station to make her official statement. But he wouldn't be surprised if the thefts and the vandalism were connected.

"You're awfully quiet."

Emerson's voice fired a thrill through the broken-down wall lying in rubble at the base of his heart. He snuck a quick glimpse at his passenger again. She held a square, covered-glass dish propped on her lap. While the aroma summoned memories of Thanksgivings as a boy, before Clint Wells had deserted his wife and young son, he hadn't been able to identify the mouthwatering food it contained.

He pushed aside the vivid recollection of his childhood, when life was simpler and family was sacred. "Sorry, work matters."

Soon the Sweetwater Bed & Breakfast loomed ahead of them where it glowed from within, creating an idyllic picture-postcard setting.

Emerson shifted in her seat, close enough that he was able to discern the gold flecks in the sincerity of her deep brown eyes.

"No thinking about work for tonight." Her voice was soft and understanding.

Refusing to be a spoilsport, he adopted a crooked grin as he tilted his Stetson toward her. "Yes, ma'am."

The action elicited a playful swat from Emerson, her laughter sluicing over him as he exited the driver's side. Opening the passenger door, he held his breath as he presented his arm.

As if they'd rehearsed the moment a thousand times, Emerson's slim fingers gripped his forearm, triggering the release of his pent-up breath.

With the glass dish balanced on her other arm, he assisted his date from the vehicle. But in the heels that she wore, when she rose to her full height, their faces were mere inches apart.

Although her dark eyes were unreadable, the twinkling string lights interspersed between the slats of the nearby overarching portico allowed a glimpse into her heart. A heart that reflected the same hope that blossomed within his.

"You made it!"

Persh's voice rang out from the inn's front porch, the sounds of merriment spilling from inside through the open door and shattering the moment.

Emerson's sharp intake of air matched his, but without missing another beat, she straightened her back and dropped her fingers from his arm. Swiveling in the direction of the B and B, she left him to hip-check the cruiser door, then trail behind. It was beyond his comprehension how he could walk on legs like jelly over their brief encounter. *Their almost kiss.*

Or at least that's the direction he'd been heading in his mind. But now, it was time to join the party, whether he was ready to or not.

After the introductions—which included plenty of oohing and aahing by the ladies over the festive attire—the adults and children gathered around the dining tables adorned with homegrown pumpkins picked from the lush gardens at the B and B, as well as garlands fashioned with leaves in hues of gold, bronze and burgundy.

An undercurrent of expectancy sizzled in the room. It thrummed through his veins. And not just because it was Thanksgiving. Rather, he attributed it to the stunning woman by his side.

The whole evening was perfect, plentiful with a delicious feast of roast turkey, stuffing, homemade cranberry sauce and every kind of imaginable side dish. Including a batch of perfectly sweet cornbread supplied by the good doctor herself.

And, of course, no gathering would be complete without an unlimited supply of the sweet water for which the inn had become famous.

He had to give Lacey credit—as well as Persh, who, no doubt, had been recruited to assist his spirited bride in delivering another celebration for the books.

He couldn't remember laughing so hard—other than the afternoon at his home stringing garland and filling up on pizza—or feeling more at ease.

At one point while seated at the dinner table, Emerson caught his eye across the place settings, the twinkle within her own conveying promise. It was then that the seedlings of hope since her arrival in town had flowered to carry him through the rest of the evening.

After the obligatory goodbyes and well-wishes had been exchanged, he barely noticed the hint of air frost as he strapped a slumbering Josie into her car seat before opening the passenger's door. His focus now centered on the woman seated next to him, he entertained thoughts of the three of them heading toward home. As a family.

Instead, he steered in the direction of the preserve. And rather than the guilt he'd occasionally wrestled with, he sensed his late wife's blessing as he peeked at the wonder of their daughter in the rearview mirror. The child who would carry on her mother's sweet love for the preserve and a zest for living.

The return drive remained silent, a bubbling of awareness simmering beneath the cloak of darkness. Once he parked the vehicle, he wiped his clammy hands against his slacks and left the engine idling. He extinguished the headlights, the solar lighting illuminating the walkway leading to the main building.

"Thank you for the ride." Emerson's voice was barely louder than a whisper. Reaching for the handle, she angled herself toward the door. "I can let myself out."

"Hold on." He bit his tongue, afraid of overstepping his bounds again. "Please." While he still didn't know the whole story, his instincts told him she'd been pushed around. And despite his overwhelming desire to protect her, he feared repeating his past missteps where she was concerned.

Emerson stilled her hand and his shoulders relaxed at her silent consent. Setting the locks in place, he then escorted her along the stone pavers that rounded the building on the way to her apartment.

"How long has that motion light been out?" Hadn't he checked all the lights?

"Sorry, I haven't paid attention." On her last word, Emerson's voice trembled. And at the threshold of her door, she fumbled for the keys in her clutch.

Memories from their first meeting swept through his mind. The faint cloud of lavender that had washed over him as she'd wriggled from his hold. Her spitfire personality he'd come to understand as more of a defense mechanism. And the unfamiliar emotions that had warred within him.

But now, shrouded in the customary sounds of the preserve, further contemplation scattered amidst the rightness of the moment. As he stepped closer still, he gulped, his breath suspended. She spun in place, her eyes like onyx, the slight catch in her throat a subtle invitation that he accepted without preamble.

Dipping his head, his lips found hers in the darkness. Chilled to the touch, they soon warmed under his.

And in that moment, Jack believed that anything was possible. Even the silly legend the townsfolk hyped. Because as far as he was concerned, there was definitely something in the sweet water when it came to Doc Parker.

Her skin tickled his small hairs as her arms tentatively looped around his neck. Emboldened, he drew her against his chest to deepen their kiss.

A slew of angry wildlife noises assaulted the night stillness and Emerson gasped, lids snapping open as she slipped her hands between them to gently push against him.

"Jack."

Confusion laced her tone. He, too, battled

the emotions stirred by their kiss, a longing to lengthen the moment. But now that he no longer held her, an urgent need to regroup took hold. An opportunity to give serious thought to what they were getting into. Because their actions involved more than just their two hearts, but also that of a child's. A child who had already suffered unimaginable loss.

Josie. He needed to get back to his daughter. Beneath the multitude of stars that flickered in contrast to the inky canvas suspended overhead, he traced the uncertainty on Emerson's face, pale in the moonlight. But he had no words of assurance to offer.

"I've got to get back to Jose." *But I want to stay.* Could she read the message in the depth of his gaze?

"Go." Her fingers fluttered like a butterfly's wings over her swollen lips before she disappeared within the safety of her apartment.

The single word hung heavy in the chilly air, its meaning undeciphered. Even still, he already regretted his next move.

Yet he still pivoted in his spot and walked away.

At some point since Jack's kiss, Emerson had lost track of the number of times her hand grazed her mouth.

But she was fully aware a blush stained her cheeks. A blush that had little to do with the color of her skin, and everything to do with Constable Jack Wells. Shaking her head, she found herself marveling at the ease in which she'd dissolved against his steadfast frame before wrapping her arms around his neck, the rhythm of their hearts falling into sync.

Wearing a silly smile, she strolled along Town Square alongside the locals and tourists enjoying the brisk fall day, barren-branched trees now lining the boulevards, their few lingering leaves scattered across the manicured lawn.

Hands buried in the pockets of her wool coat, she reflected on the holiday dinner at the inn. Without question, she'd been welcomed as family, with the Pershings serving as the perfect hosts.

Annie Greene and Josh Rogers had been there as well, which provided humorous entertainment by way of Annie's futile attempts to thwart the handsome firefighter's attention.

Marie Michaels, who wore several hats she juggled between the B and B and the church, had also attended. The woman had been integral in keeping the bed-and-breakfast's doors open following the loss of Lacey's grandparents. Alongside none other than Persh as the live-in handyman. And once Lacey and Persh had married, Marie stayed on the payroll part-time to help with bookkeeping.

Charles Bloom, the gentleman who operated the town's flower shop, had been one of the other guests invited to the dinner party.

She giggled as she remembered the shy glances the older couple exchanged, with musings of the town legend planting ideas about her own love story.

If only she could read Jack's mind.

Although she was pretty certain they'd shared the same thoughts as they'd stood in front of her apartment door.

Yet it had been three days since their kiss. And not one peep from the constable.

As Emerson tugged open the heavy wooden door leading into Sweetwater Community Church, she quickly scanned the growing crowd.

"Emerson, hi!"

Ponytail swishing over her shoulder, she locked eyes with a familiar jovial face.

"Miss Marie!"

The older woman pulled her against her soft folds, nostalgia washing over Emerson as a vision of her Aunt Francine came to mind.

"Welcome to Sweetwater Community." Marie's smile reached her eyes, which searched the nearby area. "Are you here with the constable?"

"Not today." Unbidden, a frown tugged at her lips and she nodded as Marie turned to greet another parishioner.

Had things been moving too fast between her and Jack? Or did he simply consider her a caregiver for Josie—someone he could call in a pinch as a playmate, or his stakeout partner?

Would he ever be in a place to welcome her into his heart? Or was she destined to compete with his late wife's memory?

Yet she couldn't forget the trembling of his fingers as he'd fastened her necklace, the icy blue of his eyes as they'd faced each other on the sidewalk outside of the B and B, nor the way their hearts beat as one as he kissed her with the utmost gentleness.

Perhaps his past ties kept him from moving forward, with their kiss forcing him to face the present.

Just then, Emerson spotted the man in question next to Josie—the child dressed in tights and a puffy pink down coat, her hair in the charming pigtails. Father and daughter sidled into a pew toward the front of the sanctuary adjacent to Marie, who fawned over the little girl, which did nothing to allay Emerson's fear that she was merely a stand-in or backup.

As she listened to Pastor Mark's message based on forgiveness, her heart stung with an unresolved ache. And once the service had ended, she headed toward the back doors in the hopes of avoiding Jack. She couldn't bear to be snubbed to her face.

But in her haste, she nearly bowled over Lacey.

"Is there a fire I don't know about?" Her friend chuckled, batting at her unruly coppery curls.

She observed the other woman's flushed skin, the fullness of her cheeks. *No doubt about it.* In fact, she'd stake her medical license on her certainty that Mrs. Sweetwater Pershing was expecting.

A spark of happiness comingled with a twinge in her heart. Because even though she was thrilled for the Pershings, Lacey's pregnancy also highlighted her loss and the inability to experience the same swell of new life inside of her.

Powerless to stem the tears that spilled from her eyes, she willed a sinkhole to suddenly materialize in the middle of the hallway.

"Hey… what's the matter, sweetie?" The skin beside Lacey's eyes pinched with concern as she clasped Emerson's hands with cool fingers then pulled her out of the way of others.

Shielding her eyes as she stumbled down the stairs, she battled between confessing the sordid details in the hope it would expunge her guilt, versus facing what she expected to be the other woman's horrified reaction to the truth.

A flurry of activity in the parking area captured her attention, then, as the constable and his daughter crossed in front of her line of vision.

Unable to deflect her gaze in time, she imagined Lacey would pick up on Emerson's longing for the two people who she believed could lessen the ache in her heart.

Ten minutes later, at the insistence of Lacey, she was seated in Annie's Confections & Catering and sipping a cup of decadent hot chocolate.

One of the part-time workers divided her time between the influx of Sunday-afternoon customers to periodically pause at their table to top their drinks with dollops of homemade whipped cream.

"Anytime you're ready," Lacey coaxed with an encouraging smile.

Emerson had thought she might be ready to share her reasons for moving to Sweetwater. But now she dreaded the possibility of her friend's expression transforming from compassionate to shocked.

She hesitated. *It's too soon.*

As she worried a napkin between her fingers, she considered testing the waters by gauging Lacey's reaction.

"I was in a bad relationship and thought I could fix him. Or rather…heal him." She'd accepted full responsibility for Aaron's outbursts and his unhappiness in their marriage. Assumed it must be her. Never had she crossed paths with an injured soul she hadn't been able to mend. Except for Aaron Parker.

"It was after I began counseling that I learned I don't have the power to heal everyone."

She swallowed as her final night with Aaron came back to her in living color.

No longer seated in the bakery across from Lacey, she could see herself standing in the expansive kitchen of the showpiece Aaron had purchased. Her bags were packed and hidden away, since her plan was to disappear the next morning.

But at the last minute her, ex-husband had discovered her intentions. And for the first time in their marriage, his anger had turned physical.

If a bystander peered close enough, they might notice a hint of bruising on her upper arms. But what no one could see was the life that had been growing inside of her, and that had been snuffed out in the blink of an eye.

Bringing the retelling to a close, Emerson condensed the encounter into three words.

"He struck me."

That had been just the beginning, eventually culminating in the divorce she'd begun months earlier. And ultimately into the safety of Constable Jack Wells's embrace.

And now here she was, looking at the potential of a different kind of heartbreak. One that she'd invited by permitting Jack, and Josie, into her life.

She couldn't fault them, however, not when she had been the one to plow into their lives with the intent to lighten their load.

"It wasn't your fault." Lacey's voice drew her from her thoughts. "And I don't want to overstep my bounds, but it sounds like Pastor Mark's message about forgiveness was timely."

Lacey was right. Searching her friend's gaze for condemnation or blame, she perceived only acceptance. *And love.*

If that was the case, was it possible for Jack to find it in his heart to love her, too? Of course, there was still the man's disappearing act to consider.

Which led her to the conclusion that the best thing she could do for the time being was to offer her friendship to Jack and Josie. While she continued to work through her own past hurt.

With her heart lighter than when she'd entered the bakery, she hugged Lacey goodbye, with a promise to stop by the B and B in the next few days to resume discussions about the upcoming Christmas Boutique.

When she arrived at the preserve, which closed early on Sundays, even her steps felt more carefree. As if by sharing a small part of her burden, she'd made progress toward healing.

As she twisted the key in the lock to her apartment, a strange noise on the other side of the inside wall raised the hair at the nape of her neck. She stilled, straining her ears. While she couldn't pinpoint the location, it didn't appear to be coming from the animal enclosures. Or from Dewey, who now enjoyed free range of the preserve thanks to a doggy door the maintenance staff had installed.

And since no additional attacks on the grounds had surfaced once Jack and the councilman installed the surveillance cameras, she assumed a volunteer must be straightening the gift shop. Either that, or a patron accidentally got locked inside the premises. It was also possible that one of the workers had forgotten to secure the doors.

Releasing her hold on the screen door, it closed behind her, its on-again, off-again squeak silent. When she realized Jack must've oiled the hinges, her heart warmed, and she realized that extending the gift of friendship might prove a challenge after all.

As she took off in the direction of the gift shop, she drafted a mental note to bring up safety reminders at the next staff meeting. Scanning her surroundings en route to the main building, she didn't see anything out of place. But when she reached the gift shop, she discovered the door unlatched.

Even though it didn't come as a complete surprise, it was the hard jerk on the door from the opposite side that knocked her off her feet to catapult her into a metal card rack.

She winced as the side of her face landed on the rough carpeting, one arm trapped beneath the edge of the rack. Blood thumping in her ears, she tried to distinguish the sounds around her. From her vantage point on the floor, she was unable to view her assailant—or assailants and breathed a silent prayer for protection.

"Please." Her voice quaked. "If you need money, I can open the register."

Scuffling noises met her ears, and an unpleasant, yet familiar smell filled her nostrils. Unbidden, the memories from her final standoff with Aaron slammed into her with the fury of a monsoon.

She refused to be a victim again. Pulling her arm from beneath the rack, she pushed to her knees before something slammed into her from behind.

And as she teetered at the brink of consciousness, the bizarre sounds—and the strong odor that made her think of sauerkraut—were exchanged with the sweetness of Jack's kiss.

Then everything went black.

Chapter Nine

Three days. Or more specifically, two days and fifteen-odd hours.

That was the length of time Jack had avoided Emerson like the mountainside during a lightning storm. Unless he counted his waking thoughts and nighttime dreams.

It had been their kiss.

They'd both been fully invested during the brief encounter beneath the blanket of constellations. In fact, he'd never been more mindful of his faculties than the moment their lips had touched. A precious, fragile gift.

Groaning, he scrubbed a hand through his cropped hair, the curls standing on end. Popping his Stetson in place, he chucked a form he'd been attempting to complete where it joined the litter scattered across his desk.

He could read the writing on the wall, from his failed attempts to resolve the vandalism, to parenting Josie. And now his involvement with the Christmas Boutique that Marie had lassoed him into. He was sinking fast.

No surprise. What made matters worse was the unresolved situation involving Emerson. And because it had scared the boots off him, he'd turned tail and run off in the opposite direction.

But it was still his official responsibility to alert the woman to Carley's misappropriation of the petty cash.

Chalking off the bookkeeping as a lost cause, he vacated his cubicle for the day. He stalked along the corridor of the government building, the same halls he'd walked for years. Passing the stark white walls, he let his eyes wander over the time-honored portraits of Sweetwater's founder, as well as the successive Sweetwaters who'd served on the town council.

As he neared the utilities offices, he waved at Mrs. Greer who sat at her desk. She grinned from ear to ear, returning Jack's greeting as she fluffed her snow-white bob.

Mrs. Greer had been a close friend of his mother's, often regaling Jack with stories about when, as a young boy, he became the head of his household. But rather than a sad tale, the older woman had always spun it in such a way to portray him as a hero.

Some hero.

He frowned, tallying on one hand the chaos he'd created, afraid he'd soon be adding to the other. Balling his palms into fists, he shoved them in his coat pockets and skipped down the cement stairs that descended onto the square.

A nip in the air prickled his exposed skin. With

December fast approaching, the weather had finally taken a turn. But he opted to forgo his station-issued Impala to clear his mind and pray as he walked.

Instead, however, he kept replaying the night Clint Wells had deserted his family, which had taught Jack as a young boy that he was responsible to watch over his mother. Even though it hadn't been an undertaking for a child, it had been just the two of them. And he believed that experience had equipped him to fulfill his role as constable.

Regardless, it was still his number-one priority to protect his offspring, meaning that whatever was developing between him and the vet must stop.

Because it had been Josie's innocent question as he tucked her into bed on Thanksgiving that had been his wakeup call.

"Ith Mith Em going to be my new mommy?"

Josie's inquiry and her wide eyes had taken hold of his tongue.

And since he refused to risk another loss, for either Josie or himself, he needed to clear the air with Emerson, as well as update her on the investigation. Except the more time that passed, the more awkward it became.

Hotfooting it a few blocks, he whispered prayers into the wind, his lips becoming numb.

Wait. Emerson's wool scarf. He remembered the designer wrap she'd worn to Thanksgiving dinner had fallen between the passenger seat and the console in his vehicle. The perfect ice-breaker.

He backtracked to the station, then climbed into his cruiser and nosed it toward the sanctuary.

As he turned onto the main road, his radio crackled to life, the customary static crackling across the connection.

"Incident at the preserve, all available units respond. Over."

At the location named by Josh Rogers, dread forced the breath from his lungs.

There's no way it could be related to the vandalism with a call for backup. Right?

Either way, it didn't sound good.

It helped to know Josie was safe and sound at the inn under Lacey's watch, but then Emerson's image replaced that of his daughter's. Acid sluiced through his gut.

Punching the gas pedal, he tapped his horn twice to activate the sirens and lights. With added caution, he swerved around parked cars and pedestrians as one ear listened for the all-clear.

Tires skidded upon his arrival at the preserve, then squealed as he regained traction. A knot settled in his chest cavity as he caught sight of the hook and ladder parked at an angle in front of the main building.

With his siren silent, but the strobe lights still flashing, he flung open the door before his seat belt was fully released.

Jogging toward the emergency vehicle, he watched as paramedics wheeled a stretcher from the gift shop toward a second emergency vehicle that rolled onsite and came to a stop.

Zeroing in on the gurney, which was piled high with blankets, he attempted to identify the patient. And then he glimpsed a pale cheek, eyelids closed. But it was the dark hair that gave her away.

His knees buckled and he hunched over midstride, pulling in gulps of air.

He'd arrived too late. *The story of his life.*

His role to serve and protect had been a fabrication, unable to live up to the expectations he'd adopted as a young boy. He'd eventually lost his mother, too, on the day she died.

While it had been his intent to end their developing relationship—despite his desire to build a life with Emerson—he was wracked with guilt all over again.

Because he had failed once more.

The doors to both vehicles slammed shut then rolled past him in tandem. Dust and gravel clouded the air around him, defeat closing in. Stumbling toward his cruiser, he caught Josh's voice sputtering over the radio.

"Ten-four, engine one and backup heading to Sweetwater General. Over."

Reactivating the siren, Jack buckled up. The latest report would have to wait, because right now, he needed to make sure Emerson was all right.

And with Josie's welfare a constant reminder, his decision to cut ties would be a lot easier. Or so he hoped.

As he navigated the roads, remorse washed over him for holding back about Carley's petty theft. He should have warned Emerson to keep her guard. But he and Persh had yet to piece together a correlation to the vandalism, which was weak at best. Yet with the absence of forced entry connected to each of the incidents, it continued to suggest an inside job.

And he still wrestled with the possibility that Emerson was involved in some way, especially since the vandalism had increased after her arrival.

With the traffic lights in his favor, he made good time, but it appeared the gurney had already been unloaded from the emergency vehicle.

Once he pulled into a free spot close to the hospital's entrance, with a heavy hand he shoved the vehicle into Park.

Without thinking twice, he slammed the door shut and hiked up to the automatic doors that led into the ER.

Jerking to a stop, he looked up at the sign emblazoned overhead. Sweetwater General. The hospital where Willow had lived out her last days, and the place he'd vowed never to set foot in again.

But he was here because of Emerson.

Declining to further question his motives, he

squared his shoulders and strode through the doors and up to former Councilman Spagnoletti's wife, the volunteer seated behind the desk.

"Constable Jack!" The woman patted her curly short, bright red hair. "Official business bring you in?"

"Hello, Doris." Automatically tipping his Stetson, he scanned the hallways and the open elevator car. "I'm investigating an incident related to the preserve."

Mrs. Spagnoletti instantly focused on a large computer screen that spanned the majority of her desk, long nails clacking on the keyboard.

He tapped his boot, counting the seconds until Doris looked up from her screen.

"We've got one recent arrival in CT, a Dr. Emerson Parker."

The woman's eyes, highlighted with pale blue powder, grew wide as they pivoted back to the monitor. "That's Aaron's ex-wife." Doris's curls bobbed as she again met his gaze.

"Who?" All he cared about was Emerson's condition, not a person named Aaron.

"My Harry's nephew." She lowered her voice. "You know, the developer involved in last year's scandal."

What? That news anchored in his core, pinning him to his spot. The man Emerson had been married to was linked to last year's scandal?

Did that mean his suspicions about her connection to the increased vandalism had been correct?

A jackhammer pounded against his temples.

"Thank you, Doris!" he hollered over his shoulder, as he forced his feet into action. Quickly locating the diagnostics waiting room, he claimed the chair closest to the hallway.

No more run-around. He needed answers from Emerson. Even if it shattered the remaining pieces of his heart.

Seconds turned into minutes. Perched on the edge of the chair, Stetson dangling from hands clasped in prayer, he compared himself to that drowning man.

It seemed crazy to think he'd begun to have feelings for—and even considered a future with—the former wife of the man who'd nearly torn their town apart.

If Persh—in collaboration with Josh Rogers and a favor he'd called in with Toby Witt, an old academy buddy turned PI—hadn't discovered Aaron Parker's duplicity, Harold Spagnoletti's nephew would have gotten his way.

Not surprisingly, Councilman Spagnoletti had been asked to resign from his position. Although the man had been equally shocked to learn of his nephew's nefarious actions, he'd chosen to remain in Sweetwater with both he and Doris making retribution through philanthropy.

Had Aaron Parker sent Emerson to Sweetwater

to pick up where he'd left off before the townsfolk had run him out of town?

Jack pushed his fist against his chest, massaging the boulder that was growing by epic proportions.

Finally, the double doors leading into the diagnostics wing swung open and his heart flipped as soon as he recognized the woman being pushed across the threshold.

A thin blanket draped across her body, the mahogany crown of thick hair fanning around her shoulders. At the mere sight of her, the stone in his gut dissolved.

Yet he couldn't ignore the questions he still needed answers to.

Why was she in Sweetwater? And why now?

What a fool.

Emerson had let down her guard, and not only with regard to the honorable constable and the condition of her heart. But by being preoccupied and being caught unawares by the gift shop intruders.

She gingerly touched the bandage covering the raw skin on her cheek, grateful she'd escaped with only minor injuries. According to Josh Rogers, she'd scared away the trespassers and nothing had been stolen. Except that the preserve was now closed to patrons during the ongoing investigation.

A sigh shuddered through her at the reality that her home and position were both in jeopardy.

"Oh, no, Dewey!" His urgent barking hovered at the periphery of her memory. One consolation came in the form of a promise that volunteers would still continue to show up at the preserve. But she wouldn't mind the dog's comforting presence amid the beeping machines and the sterile atmosphere.

Imagining Jack's reaction to the bandage on her face and the IV attached to her arm, Emerson was flooded with weariness. But in light of his absence for the past few days, she didn't hold out hope that he'd turn up.

Seconds later, however, she received her answer as Sweetwater's constable barged into the room, storm clouds churning behind his eyes.

Experience had schooled her to cower in similar situations, yet she sensed Jack's behavior was more like that of her father's when faced with concern or worry. Instinctively, her heart squeezed toward the man towering over her.

"I'm okay." Her voice squeaked. And even though she should've called 911 at the first hint of an intruder, she refused to let Jack assume fault for her injuries.

"I'm pulling you off surveillance detail."

Jack worried the Stetson between his hands, a coping mechanism she'd witnessed often. Her fingers twitched, itching to smooth his unruly curls into place near the downy softness at the nape of his neck.

What did he just say?

"Excuse me?" Attempting to hoist herself upright in the hospital bed, the movement jarred her ribs and she flinched.

His arms crossed over his chest like a sentry, Jack's expression brooked no argument.

"I'll bring in someone else to take over for you."

His tone flat and final, she tamped down her wily defenses. Now wasn't the time to fight back. It was Jack's jurisdiction and he was calling the shots.

"You know best." Turning her head to hide the disappointment coursing through her, she recalled her earlier resolve to offer friendship to Jack and his daughter. But whether or not he accepted was his choice.

The silence stretched between them, and when she turned back, she knew there was no changing his mind.

Especially when he spun on his heel and walked away. Again.

With preparations underway and wares to be crafted for the town's annual Christmas Boutique, Emerson was thankful for the extra work to keep her hands and mind busy.

Deftly securing the end of the baby blanket,

she set the cloud of yarn in front of her. "All finished." Did her smile come off as forced as it felt?

She was seated at one of the inn's dining tables embellished with Christmas baubles and colorful candy canes, gaily adorned packages and holly and berries. Also replacing the autumn directions, cinnamon-and-spice-scented pine cones were scattered throughout the living area, and the added festiveness helped buoy her spirits.

"Anyone for seconds?" Bustling from the kitchen through the swinging door, Lacey carried a pitcher filled to the brim with the legendary sweet-tasting ice water.

Although Emerson was certain the beverage wreaked havoc on her mental capacities, that didn't stop her from holding up her empty tumbler. "Oh, why not?"

A giggle escaped and she slapped her hand over her mouth.

It turned out that the more she consumed of the sweet concoction, the more vulnerable her heart became toward the undisputedly difficult yet rugged constable, who she'd only seen in passing since her overnight hospital stay.

Lacey winked at her as she filled her glass. "You know what they say…" she said with a smile.

"There's something in the sweet water!" the women said in unison.

"So, what's happening on the preserve front?" Annie set down the flour sacks she was embroidering with intricate details and playful sayings stitched into the fabric. *Coffee and Jesus. Sweet tooths are welcome.* And several other charming quotes.

Emerson swallowed a sip of the iced water then set her crochet hook on the shiny walnut-topped table. "Constable Jack assigned someone to help patrol the grounds."

Upon spotting the cruiser recently, her pulse had jumped, before the crush of disappointment quickly settled in when it had been someone other than Jack behind the wheel.

"And still no vandalism or otherwise since yours truly interrupted the latest excitement."

Marie shuddered from across the table. "That must've been incredibly frightening."

The older woman peered over her reading glasses, eyes awash with compassion. But Emerson preferred not to relive that afternoon, and instead reveled in the peace that had consumed her minutes before help arrived.

Although it hadn't been in the form she'd hoped, she told herself it had been for the best that Jack hadn't been the one on scene. Not after she'd witnessed his reaction at her bedside.

"I'm just glad it's behind me, even though the surveillance footage was undecipherable." Pasting another smile on her face, she grabbed a fresh skein of yarn to begin stitching a new baby blanket. It was a skill she'd taught herself when she'd learned she was expecting.

But once she lost her baby, she'd packed away her yarn for good. Until she discovered that working with the soft fibers was therapeutic. She'd even begun to contemplate that one day she may fully divulge the rest of her story from that fateful night.

And it seemed that time may be now, as an inner prompting invited her to finally find forgiveness and move forward.

Perhaps each moment during the last several weeks had been preparing her to love again, but was Constable Jack the man to fill that role?

Not until he was ready and willing to put his past behind him.

"That is a lovely blanket, dear."

As Marie rubbed the soft material of variegated hues in pale yellow, green and orange between her fingers, her knowing gaze compelled Emerson to finish sharing her account.

In turn, she gazed at each of the ladies who'd become her closest friends. As if anticipating the significance of the moment, Lacey, Annie and Marie put aside their projects, and gave her their undivided attention.

"It was the final night with my ex-husband. Aaron." Prepared to confront the pain and self-inflicted guilt, she revisited that horrible place in her memories, barely registering Lacey's gentle touch against her forearm.

"The yelling had been nothing new, but I'd pushed him over the edge—" She cut herself off as she heard her therapist's reminder. It had been Aaron's lack of self-control that triggered the unfolding tragedy, not anything Emerson had done.

"Aaron was furious when he discovered my plans to leave." Recoiling, she clutched her abdomen as she relived those minutes. "He struck me and I fell against our granite countertop."

Silence descended as three pairs of eyes fixed on her.

"I remember Aaron kicking a chair. Then it slammed into my side and I crumpled to the floor." She paused to coat her parched throat.

What happened in succession was harder for her to put into context with so much of it a blur. The gun she fired. A bullet grazing Aaron's shoulder.

"The following morning, my nurse at the hospital told me the baby I'd been carrying didn't survive." Half-hiccupping, half-sobbing, she dabbed at tears that threatened to spill.

It was the next part of her story that she skipped, how she'd hemorrhaged and almost died. And that the emergency surgery had saved her life, but it had also sealed her fate.

She'd never bear children of her own.

"How did you end up here?" Lacey's voice interrupted the quiet.

Once she'd been released from the hospital, Emerson had returned to a blessedly empty home. "I'd conducted research and interviewed for the veterinarian position at the preserve well in advance. So I grabbed my bag and disappeared."

She could see it now, that every detail leading up to her arrival in town had been divinely orchestrated. Even these women were an answer to prayer. And even if he didn't know it, so was the constable.

"I filed my divorce papers and checked into a hotel for a couple weeks to regain my strength. And now here I am." She exhaled, depleted yet liberated.

Lacey, Annie and Marie gathered around her and drew her close. Their compassion and acceptance instigated a fresh batch of tears to wet her cheeks.

"That's a lot for one person to live with," Marie said as they released her.

A burgeoning sense of relief washed over her. Mopping her face with a tissue, she sniffled. "It has been, but I'm ready to heal and…"

Dare she voice it aloud?

"And?" Annie asked, powdered sugar clinging to her lips from one of the sweet-and-sour lemon bars she'd brought from the bakery for their afternoon of crafting.

"Possibly love again."

She said it, the words sparking three ridiculous and matching grins that did wonders to lighten the mood.

"What?" She screwed up her face.

"Don't give up on him, er, it…"

When Lacey coughed behind her napkin, Emerson swatted her arm.

"I'm not holding my breath where the constable is concerned." She backed up her words by expelling a sigh. "But I know a little girl whom I've become awfully attached to." After inhaling a lungful of air, she blew it out again. "I may have to be content with that."

But the visits with the constable's daughter had ceased, too.

Yet stranger things had happened. After all, if the town legend could be believed, then true love would prevail.

"Just in case, though, you might need to supply Constable Jack with a gallon of your proprietary iced water." And then she laughed, her heart soaring with promise as it had when she'd been a little girl, and the mamma bird returned to its baby.

With unabashed glee, Emerson presented her glass for thirds.

"Say, speaking of the constable." Lacey started packing up her craft supplies. "With the preserve temporarily closed, is it still okay if I bring Josie by to visit Dewey?"

"Oh, he would love that…and so would I!" How she looked forward to spending time with Jack's daughter. The rescue pooch had done a number on her heart, too. And since he'd healed up, she'd been working on training him.

One additional thing for her to focus on. Besides her hope for more than friendship with a certain strawberry-blond lawman.

Chapter Ten

When Jack had spotted Emerson lying on the gurney at the hospital, her skin pale against the backdrop of rich, dark hair, it had ignited a maelstrom of emotions he'd stuffed away at the time.

But he could trace a good portion of them to his previous encounter at Sweetwater General.

He hadn't walked the halls of the medical complex since saying his goodbyes to his late wife. And he wouldn't have returned if official business hadn't forced his hand.

The experience had been like stepping into the past, from the onslaught of antiseptic smells bitter with traces of artificial fragrance, to the sterile decor and beeping monitors tracking patients' vitals, to voices muddled over the hospital's intercom.

But this time he'd shown up for the veterinarian who'd threatened to steal his heart—lock, stock and precinct-issued barrel.

Until Josie had asked if Emerson was going to be her new mommy. And despite his desire to explore the possibility of a relationship with the woman, he'd failed to protect her from an unknown assailant where she lived and worked.

Granted, a sudden illness hadn't been involved

this time around. But it had still occurred on his watch. And the safety measures he'd enacted—from the cameras, to added security to his covert off-hours patrol—should've been enough to keep her from harm.

Swiping a hand over his stubble, Jack couldn't shake the defiance that had flashed in Emerson's eyes when he'd pulled her off the stakeouts. And because the station didn't have the money to bring on anyone else, he was driven to borrow from his personal funds until he could figure out a better way.

It was either that or stand back and watch the council close down the preserve permanently. And that was out of the question.

"Guess what, Daddy?" Josie's little voice perked up from the back seat, pulling Jack from his whirl-wind of thoughts.

He peered at his daughter in the rearview mir-ror, her pigtails lopsided.

"Mith Lathey is taking me to thee Mith Em and Dewey!"

And there it was again. The innocent reference to Doc Parker thrust his thinking right back to the rabbit trail that now began and ended with her.

"That sounds like a lot of fun, Jose." He forced the big ol' familiar lump down his throat.

If only circumstances could be different. That they could somehow…

Stop it. He'd experienced his one true love.

And after his stint at Emerson's hospital bed-side, he'd grabbed onto her ex-husband's ties with the developer as his defense. Never mind that he had no intention of risking loss again.

Once was enough.

The idyllic community, his church family and caring friends who rallied around him and Josie would need to be sufficient.

He shifted the cruiser into Park and shut off the engine. Because of budget cuts and red tape, the annual tree-lighting ceremony scheduled for earlier in the month had been postponed. But just that morning, a thin layer of the season's first real snowfall had greeted the town. Which was perfect timing for the rescheduled lighting.

With a bonus dip in temperatures, the antici-pation of a white Christmas was hard not to feel despite the burdens he shouldered.

Carrying Josie up the sidewalk in front of the bed-and-breakfast, Jack left tracks in his wake. He planned to tackle a few things at the office before the two of them—along with Lacey and Persh—would join hundreds of residents and visitors for the long-awaited shindig held in Town Square.

Would a dark-haired veterinarian make an ap-pearance as well?

Once Josie's feet lit on the wooden planks in-side the inn, he kissed the top of her flyaway hair before Lacey led his daughter to the sofa, with a brand-new *Coconut the Chimp & His Adventures* book in hand.

She dismissed him with a wave toward the back of the property—a silent invitation to stop at the Lodge, a large A-frame building near the overflow parking.

Not long after the Pershings had married, the couple converted the structure into an after-school hangout for young boys and teens who came from troubled homes.

He admired his buddy's ability to split his time between his onsite handiwork and teaching real-world skills to the young men they hosted. Even more importantly, to live out his faith—and how to be a man—by example. It was something Persh had lacked after his mom passed away and his dad emotionally checked out, ultimately leaving Persh to fend for himself.

It had been Lacey's grandparents—Gram and Pops Sweetwater—who'd offered young Persh a job, schooling him in the same concepts he shared with the boys growing up in similar households. Although both Jack's circumstances and his buddy's had been different, they shared a decades-long kinship through mutual understanding.

And then when Lacey returned to town with the intent to sell off her inheritance of the B and B, he'd had the privilege of wearing his other hat as legal counsel. With all that had transpired concerning the senior Sweetwater's amended last will and testament, it was nothing short of divine intervention when the couple ended up together, substantiating the validity of the town legend.

He sighed. *If only.*

Once the two had reunited, along with Persh's extra responsibilities as town councilman, he'd also converted the Lodge's upstairs apartment—the same space he'd occupied for years—into a safe place for any of the boys requiring it.

In addition, over the past year, the Pershings had opened up the facility on Wednesday evenings for a contemporary worship jam session free to the public.

Yet despite his beautiful life, with Josie his biggest blessing, a twinge of envy weighted down his boots as he entered the Lodge's main level.

"Hey, buddy." Persh lifted a hand in greeting.

Releasing a low whistle, Jack admired the councilman's craftsmanship. "I see you got yourself roped into the boutique business, too." He chuckled. "Miss Marie?"

"It was actually Red's…er, my wife's idea." The slip of Lacey's nickname and the twinkle in his eye belied his mock-irritation.

With a steady hand, Persh applied white paint to a section of palm bark. After setting the brush on a portable workbench, he shoved his stool back then pointed at the piles of additional bark. "When I drove into Phoenix last weekend, Lacey instructed me to hit the suburbs ripe with palm trees and gather as much as I could."

Rising to his full height, Persh stretched his back and laughed. "Of course I had no idea why until today."

Selecting one of the finished pieces, Jack examined the charming addition to the boutique. Persh had added long black fringe for lashes and round black pupils to the huge, oval-shaped white eyeballs. And big red pom-poms, hot-glued onto the bark, mimicked Rudolph's red nose. The matching split, frayed sections of bark served as deer antlers.

"I just have to make bows with the scraps of material over there." Persh pointed to his work area. "Then hot-glue those to pine cones Lacey collected from our property, attach them to the antlers and voilà." He waved his hand at the half-dozen deer heads he'd already assembled.

"Times fifty if I know Lacey Sweetwater Pershing." Jack's laughter mingled with his friend's as he slapped a hand against his thigh. He'd missed the easy camaraderie, his drama taking up too much of his time lately.

Persh returned to the bench, inviting Jack to sit on a second stool. But he remained standing due to piles of paperwork at the station that required his attention.

"Say, anything conclusive from the cameras

when Doc Parker was injured?" He didn't even try to feign nonchalance.

Persh swiped at the perspiration popping out on his hairline from the heat radiating from the overhead lighting.

"Sorry to say, Jack, but the feed was a royal blur." He scrunched his eyebrows together. "The strangest part was that whoever was on the other side of the camera seemed to be playing with it."

What on earth? "What do you make of it?"

"I was hoping you'd have a better idea since you're the law." Persh chuckled.

You would think so. "Maybe I'm just too close to the situation." He couldn't deny that it had always been personal. But Emerson's involvement—either intentionally or unintentionally—only upped the stakes.

"Hey, you still planning to attend tonight's lighting ceremony?" Persh grabbed the hot-glue gun and affixed several pine cones.

"I wouldn't miss it, but work is calling now." While Persh might ordinarily tell him not to answer that particular call, without the extra funds, there was no other way around it.

Jack clapped his buddy on the shoulder, then exited the Lodge and made his way through the backyard, taking in the cozy setup for guests to enjoy on the back patio. He couldn't get over the efforts his friends had invested to bring the bed-and-breakfast back from financial ruin. And all that work had paid off. Today, it was a thriving business listed in the National Register of Historic Places.

Upon his arrival at the station, he immersed himself in the stacks of bookkeeping, the time passing quickly. When he came up for a breath and noticed the late hour, it made more sense for him to meet Persh, Lacey and Josie at Town Square, rather than return to the inn.

And with parking congestion at a record high during the holidays and special events, keeping his car parked at the station ensured convenient access once the ceremony was over. That way, he'd be able to transport Miss Josie home before her coach turned into a pumpkin.

He stifled a yawn. Even though it was nowhere near midnight, his prolonged late evenings and early mornings continued to take a toll. But one thing was in his favor: he'd learned earlier in the day that Carley had willingly agreed to stop at the station to talk. And even though the surveillance video proved inconclusive as far as Emerson's attack, he wanted a statement before pointing fingers—praying the vandalism would cease once a probable suspect was identified.

After locking up his files, he set out for Town Square, the snow still coating the ground. Once the case was solved, he hoped to plan a road adventure with Josie during her summer break from school. Maybe a month-long sightseeing trip through the central part of the states into the Midwest. He'd heard that the Land of 10,000 Lakes was lush and scenic at that time of year.

His phone dinged, alerting him to a text.

Who was he kidding? When was the last time he'd even taken more than a consecutive day off?

As he milled among the gathering crowd surrounding the expansive roped-off area—compliments of the volunteer tree-lighting committee—he grabbed his cell phone from his jacket pocket. His pulse leaped into his throat as he read the cryptic message from Persh. Josie's okay. Running late. Will explain.

Okay, now what? It was a phrase that was becoming all too common in his vocabulary.

"You're certain I should bring Josie to the lighting?" Emerson repeated the question for the fourth time.

And each response from Lacey and Persh had been the same. "He needs to see for himself she's okay."

While she doubted her friends' logic, they both shared a longtime history with the constable and knew him better than she did. She'd also been the one to care for Josie's injuries since Persh had needed Lacey's assistance with the evening's arrangements.

"Will Daddy be mad?" Josie's eyes, startling

in their resemblance to her father's, clouded with worry that no five-year-old should have had.

Gathering Jack's daughter into the shelter of her arms, Emerson held her tight as if she was her own child. She wouldn't even try to mask her fierce love for the child, the wee one a balm to her heart.

Cradling Josie against her, she inhaled the scent of sugar cookies and bubblegum-scented shampoo before choosing her words with care. "No, he won't be mad." She thought back to her own father's reactions as she was growing up. "But it might seem like it because sometimes daddies act that way when they're sad. Or scared."

"Really?" The child's bow lips pursing, she didn't seem convinced,.

"I promise." After planting a kiss on the little girl's injured arm, she explained to her that when she was young—right around Josie's age—she used to pretend she was a horse and gallop through the house. But oftentimes her long hair, flowing free from her braid, would catch on the back of a chair or a door handle, causing her dad to scowl.

What she came to learn over time was that concern had put those creases on her father's face, rather than anger. But what she didn't tell Josie was how she'd witnessed that very same response when her mother had died in a car accident that left him to raise her as a single dad, alongside her Aunt Francine.

She tweaked Josie's button nose. "Plus, we'll tell your daddy it was an accident."

The child sighed as she pressed her warm body closer to Emerson, giggling as Dewey shoved his velvety snout between them.

As she scratched the dog behind his ears with her free hand, the story she'd relayed to Josie took on a whole new meaning. Because even though she'd oftentimes attributed her ex-husband's heated outbursts to fear or concern for far too long, it was now that she finally accepted that Aaron's temper stemmed from deep-seated issues beyond her control.

"I'm thorry 'bout what happened."

Josie's sweet voice tugged at Emerson's heartstrings. "I know, honey, and it's all forgiven." One minute, she and Lacey had been walking and talking on the preserve grounds, and the next, Josie's high-pitched scream had pierced the air.

In that moment, her heart had pounded harder than during her attack in the gift shop. And without hesitation, the two of them had bolted toward the direction of the child's cry.

But as commonly happened with children and adults alike, Jack's daughter had been more frightened than hurt.

Yet, neither woman really understood what had occurred. According to Josie, she'd been feeding the spider monkeys—Monte and Molly—before ending up knee-deep in manure inside Louie the llama and Alvin the alpaca's joint pen.

Careful to minimize the transfer of muck onto their clothing, they'd carried a whimpering Josie to the clinic.

Assuming her doctor persona once in the exam room, Emerson had cleaned up her patient from head to toe, relieved to discover only a few minor scratches and a mildly sprained wrist. To be on the safe side, though, she'd taken X-rays, breathing a sigh of relief when her suspicions were confirmed.

Josie supported her bandaged arm in the sling, her little eyebrows drawn together in concentration. "Daddy might not let me come here anymore." She pouted, then hung her head.

Heart squeezing with compassion, Emerson pressed her lips to the top of the child's head, the fine hairs tickling her nose. "Oh, sweetheart, it'll be okay once we tell your daddy it was an accident."

She grabbed an extra coat that Lacey had the foresight to bring when the two had showed up earlier. "Here, let's put your jacket on."

Dewey barked, tail wagging.

Josie's face lit up, her worries all but forgotten. "Look, Dewey wanth to come!"

And that's exactly what they did. After the clinic was locked up, the three of them set course for Town Square.

Where she would eventually encounter a fine-looking, protective and equally evasive constable. Whom she missed terribly.

Since the night she'd appeared at the Wells's cottage to discuss the surveillance plans—what now seemed a lifetime ago—she'd sensed an undercurrent of something developing between them, certain in the days that followed that they were teetering on the cusp of something promising.

Except that now they weren't even on speaking terms.

With Josie settled in the car seat that Lacey left with Emerson, and Dewey situated next to the child in the back seat, both radiated equal amounts of energy. Whether Jack admitted it or not, the dog would make a wonderful addition to their little family.

Yet that idea did little to settle Emerson's racing nerves as she mentally practiced how to tell him Josie had been injured in her care. Especially after the man's behavior at her hospital bedside.

"There he ith—Daddy!" From her spot in the back seat, Josie pointed toward the gathering throng.

Thankful that the Pershings had provided explicit instructions on where to find Jack waiting, she cautiously navigated the vehicle through the crowded street. Her pulse stuttered at the flash of a Stetson propped atop the head of the stocky officer.

And with the way he paced, it appeared Jack was going to drive a rut through the snow-packed ground near the gazebo—the structure a home base for musical ensembles held throughout the spring and summer, as well as the town's holiday celebrations and special events.

As they crawled along the street, a parking spot opened adjacent to the square. Exiting the coziness of the car's interior, her nose tingled due to the dropping temperatures.

Before leaving the clinic, she'd searched for her wool scarf, but then recalled it had been missing since the Thanksgiving dinner.

Tucking the hood of her coat around her ears, she unlatched the straps to the car seat. "Here you go."

Straightening Josie's stocking cap, she collected the child and clutched Dewey's leash with her free hand. Then she clicked her key fob, before closing the doors behind them and heading toward the festivities.

Dewey yipped, his tongue lolling as he shared the crowd's excitement. There was so much to take in, the wintry scene highlighted by a mass of event-goers lining the cordoned street and sidewalk.

Comfortable with multitasking, Emerson maneuvered through the hustle and bustle with ease,

Josie firmly nestled against her side with one arm, her other hand gripping the leash.

But as soon as Jack's gaze zeroed in on her, she tripped over an invisible crack in the pavement. As if she'd forgotten how to put one foot in front of the other. Righting herself without further incident, she surveyed Josie's father as he closed the distance between them.

She pressed a fist to her chest, which did nothing to still her racing heart as she observed the pinched skin near his eyes, and his lips in a straight line. Lips that had met hers with a feather-light touch.

But it was his parental concern that now rolled off him in currents.

His ice-blue gaze remained trained on hers as he pushed his way among the horde. Until they were so close the scent of his musky aftershave washed over her, the faint freckles scattered along the bridge of his nose visible in the square's twinkling lights.

"Daddy!" Josie extended her unrestrained arm toward her father.

Jack reached out and drew his daughter against him, his eyes fixed on the sling that hugged her injured limb.

Wincing, his throat worked with something akin to anger or fear. Or a combination of both.

"It's just a sprain," Emerson whispered to Jack,

his eyes averted as he squeezed Josie close, careful to avoid her wounded wrist.

"It wath an acthident, Daddy." She patted Jack's face, triggering a half sob, half chuckle to erupt from his throat.

It was all Emerson could do not to throw her arms around the two of them. But it was not her place. And there was also the matter of a very eager and very energetic puppy that tugged hard at his leash.

Ruff!

"Dewey, quiet." Speaking with an authoritative tone, she pulled a treat from her coat pocket. One of several simple commands taught at a course she'd attended early in her career.

While she hoped that Jack would adopt the pooch into his household, she wouldn't force the issue. After all she'd never intended to adopt an animal herself.

Yet Dewey had effortlessly wheeled his way into her heart, alongside the constable and his daughter. The staff was pretty taken with him as well.

Of course, Josie would always be welcome to visit anytime.

The sudden awareness of Jack's scrutiny launched a flush to heat her cheeks before she pushed the hood off her head.

"I'm so sorry Lacey and I lost track of Josie." Even though children could be notorious for wandering off, that was no excuse. "And then our girl slipped off the wooden fence."

His eyes were unwavering, still focused on her. "I'm not sure who was more surprised—Louie or Alvin!"

"It wath my fault!" Josie tugged on her father's Stetson.

And her earlier nerves at telling Jack what happened was replaced with a need to erase the concern marring his skin.

"Lacey texted me. I know what happened."

The gruffness in Jack's voice belied the relief evident in the relaxation of his jaw, where dark stubble dotted the surface.

"Okay, then." A stiffness filled the space between them.

"I guess I'll be going." And then Lacey and Persh approached, big smiles on their faces as they waved. But she had no intention of playing the fifth wheel.

Jack lowered Josie to the ground and the sprite stomped across the snowy ground. Dewey tugged at his leash, eager to follow.

Brightening the area were tiny globe lights strung across the gazebo, as well as the trees lining the walkway leading up to the steps of the courthouse building, making it easier to recognize familiar faces. After a quick peek at the man next to her, and confirmation that his attention was glued to his daughter, she applied pressure to the leash and attempted to slip away.

"Emerson."

Before she'd taken more than two steps, Jack's deep voice thrummed through her veins. Stopping midstride, she craned her neck and read the confusion within the deep lines around his mouth.

A charge of awareness bridged the chasm that separated them.

"Please. Stay."

With three strides, he spanned the invisible lines that had been drawn, warmth radiating from him.

Her pulse leaped against her neck and she swallowed hard. Because what she wanted, and what he was asking, were two very different things.

Because she wanted far more than simply staying for a tree lighting.

But could it be a start?

Before she was able to answer her own question, Dewey took advantage of her distraction and pulled from her grasp before bounding in Josie's direction. He reached her just as the child's Uncle Persh scooped her into his arms.

Both him and Lacey sported identical smiles as they gaped at her and Jack, tempting her to put a stop to their wayward thinking.

But that's when a hush fell over the entire square, and the Sweetwater Community College marching band began belting out a familiar holiday tune.

A collective cheer from the attentive audience rose around her before young and old voices blended together. And the last vestiges of tension lifted as she joined in, hands clapping in time with the bass drum.

Until the largest fir tree that she'd ever seen, aside from any gracing the front side of a postcard, suddenly blinked on with thousands of lights. Transfixed, she remained rooted in place. And just like that, Town Square transformed into an enchanted wonderland.

Because with her eyes glued to the Christmas tree, it was easy to believe that wishes—and legends—might still come true. Even for her.

Chapter Eleven

Holding a zonked-out Josie against his chest, Jack stepped across the threshold into his cottage. He also held onto the hope that Emerson hadn't read anything more in to his invitation to stay for the tree lighting other than a thank-you.

But once the ceremony had ended, and everyone had said their goodbyes, there was no mistaking the glimmering gold flecks dancing in her deep brown eyes. A look that conveyed expectation as she gazed at him and his daughter.

Before the tree lighting had even begun, though, he'd been waiting for Persh and Lacey to show up with Josie. He'd been reflecting on Christmastime in Sweetwater, and how he'd worked hard each year to create happy memories for Josie. And even though that year was no exception, he'd also been entertaining the possibility of new traditions, with Emerson at the forefront.

Yet the mounting suspicion involving her past and the unsolved vandalism, and his unwillingness to risk another loss, had forced him to keep the doc at a distance. Except at the heart of it all, it really came down to avoiding the one thing he didn't deserve.

Emerson's love.

And then he'd received the cryptic text from Persh, which had triggered another bout of indigestion.

But once he'd called the bed-and-breakfast, and Persh had alleviated his unease, Lacey followed up with a detailed explanation that corroborated Emerson's story.

Cautious to a fault, he'd still needed to examine his child to ensure another trip to Sweetwater General could be avoided.

The wait for Josie to arrive had been interminable, the ache in his stomach the result of regret—for entrusting her care to others, and for failing to protect someone else close to him.

It had been impossible to enjoy the happenings around him as he tried with little success to redirect his train of thought, absently skimming over the tinsel garlands and oversize candy canes dyed in red, green and white that bedecked the storefronts along Main Street.

Shifting from one booted foot to the other, he'd observed the community band members preparing to perform. Hands shoved in his pockets, his eyes had been peeled for Josie and the Pershings.

But then Emerson had stepped into his view, her dark hair lustrous and face lit by the twinkling luminaries that dripped from ponderosas and aspens, his daughter safely tucked against her. Sucking in a quick breath, he had steeled himself to square off with the woman for the first time since his hospital call. His eyes flitted over her cheek and the near-invisible blemishes that remained from the attack.

At the sight of the pair, Dewey tagging alongside, the ache in his chest had intensified with his yearning to create a family. Except that her ex-husband's involvement with the town scandal had left too many unanswered questions.

A shuddering sigh had rolled through him as he returned to the bottom line and his inability to protect his daughter.

But as he'd held Josie, Emerson a hairbreadth away, he'd wanted nothing more than to extend his gratitude to her. The best he'd been able to come up with had been to invite her to stay for the tree lighting.

The crowds had faded into the background, then, and the Pershings had moved to the periphery of their small group, which had lent an intimacy to the wonderland. Their arms had brushed together as townsfolk milled past, his hand hovering near hers. Adam's apple bobbing, he'd stifled the urge to span the distance and intertwine his fingers with hers. But he'd refused to plant more ideas in Josie's mind, along with questions he wasn't prepared to answer.

Yet what about Emerson? Did he want to give her ideas?

Regardless of his longing to protect her with the potential for more, a question still haunted him. *Could he trust her?*

Early the next afternoon, Jack had nearly worn a hole into the already threadbare carpeting where he paced outside Sweetwater's government offices.

He'd shown up to wait for an unscheduled one-on-one with Councilman Drew Pershing following a fitful night of tossing and turning like a trapped animal, his dreams plagued with visions of a raven-haired veterinarian lying on a gurney that Josie teetered on as it whizzed down a nearby butte. And he had a pretty good idea his appearance ranked up there with as bad as he felt.

As he whispered a prayer for guidance, Persh emerged from his office and extended his hand. Popping his Stetson on his head, Jack followed his buddy into the small room, then took a seat in the only available chair.

"By the hefty size of those under-eye bags, this must be important." Persh latched the door and settled into the wingback behind his metal desk.

After plucking a piece of crumpled paper from his shirt pocket and smoothing it right-side up on the notepad in front of Persh, Jack propped his elbows on the desktop.

"Read it." His words, like his heart, were coated in angst.

"You're quitting?" Persh pounded a fist on the surface, toppling a picture frame. Pinching the bridge of his nose with his thumb and forefinger, he frowned at Jack.

He averted his eyes. Had he made the right decision? It wasn't like he'd resigned without careful consideration. And because his role involved protecting Sweetwater's welfare, he justified his actions. He believed it was in the town's best interests to bring in someone better suited for the job. Someone who could successfully separate their work and home lives.

His pager buzzed. Squinting, he read the number.

"Hold on, I need to make a call." Grabbing his cell, he punched in the number for Sweetwater Preserve & Sanctuary. And because he'd never received a page originating from the preserve, it activated his overactive imagination.

After the first ring, his call was picked up and he hit the speaker.

"Jack."

Emerson.

It wasn't just frustration that laced her tone, but it was in the subsequent pause that he sensed her valiant effort to feign bravado.

"What happened?"

"More destruction." A sob broke free over the connection.

The attacks had slowed to a crawl during the

past week or so, but apparently it had been only a reprieve. And now, a new report would need to be filed. But by turning in his resignation, the responsibility was no longer his.

Forcing the acid back down his throat, he vowed to continue fighting to save the preserve. He'd just have to find another way.

"I'll get someone out there as soon as possible." His words were clipped and to the point.

Silence rang in his ears. *Was she still there?*

"You're safe?" Guilt stung as he shoved away his niggling suspicions over her involvement.

"Yes." She paused. "I'm in my apartment now."

While that familiar draw to ensure her safety near dragged him from Persh's office, the piece of paper in the councilman's hand said otherwise.

Had she said goodbye before the call ended? With the weight of his buddy's scrutiny, he couldn't be sure.

"You can't resign." His tone tempered, Persh sliced a hand through his hair, tugging at the ends in anguish.

"Too late." Reaching toward his badge, his fingers skimmed across the vacant spot that once held the gold band he'd worn these past three years. He yanked the badge from his collar then plunked it onto the middle of the desk, the metal edges pressing into his palm.

It had been prior to his impromptu meeting with Persh that he'd penned the missive clutched in the councilman's tight grip. But even before he'd arrived at the courthouse building, he'd made a stop at the pawn shop located on Main Street, across from Town Square.

Removing the wedding band from its placeholder, he'd relinquished it to Mr. Timmons, the owner of Twice-Loved Treasures.

It had felt like he'd been paying his respects all over again as he parted with the ring. There'd been no guilt, only a well of sadness that he wouldn't be presenting it to Josie on her eighteenth birthday.

But he'd had no choice. It had been the only logical way to maintain the town's best interests, and thereby fulfill his duty to serve. And to protect.

Because even though it was a simple gold band, as an heirloom it had garnered ample funds to hire the patrolling security guard to replace Jack until the town council could fill his vacant position.

And as Mr. Timmons plucked the band from his calloused palm, it was as if he'd finally taken the first step to put his past to rest.

Persh's gaze zeroed in on his barren collar, angst replaced by concern. "I don't know what's going on, my friend. But you need to call in a favor and get someone on scene. And stat."

He pushed out of his seat with new resolve. *What harm would it do to take one last report?*

"But that person is not you." Persh's tone brooked no argument.

Jack stilled, tugging on his ear as if to clear it. "Excuse me?"

"You heard right. Take off the rest of today. We'll discuss this—" he waved the paper in the air "—conversation in the morning."

Isn't this what he'd wanted?

When it must've appeared to Persh that he wasn't going to budge, the councilman rounded his desk to escort Jack to the door.

In a daze, he wound a scarf around his neck before stepping onto the courthouse steps. Snow flurries fell lightly from the overcast sky. Out of habit, his fingers lingered on his bare collar, causing his knees to buckle.

This might very well have been the biggest blunder of his lifetime.

Maybe not turning in his resignation, but by thinking he was the one in control.

With a million thoughts swirling through his mind, Jack grasped the railing to keep from taking a spill like the snowflakes that drifted around him.

Making his way down the stairs, images flashed through his mind. Josie playing in the "white stuff" on the church grounds, catching the flakes that fell on the tip of her tongue. The three of them rolling a snowman together in the backyard at his cottage.

Followed by the developer that had bulldozed into town and the subsequent trouble at the B and B, and then the situation at the preserve. Finally, his legs could no longer carry the pressing weight upon his shoulders.

Falling to his knees, the dampness seeped through the denim as snow blanketed him like a cocoon.

"I'm so confused." He bowed his head, the faces of those he'd failed throughout his lifetime passing behind his eyes. His mother, Grace. He choked back a cry. She would've denied it, of course, never uttering an unkind word in all the years that he'd known her. Not even when her husband had deserted them to live with his secret family, which had placed Jack in charge as a child.

He'd struggled to keep his mother safe, while Grace took whatever odd jobs she could find to retain a roof over their heads and food on the table. Despite the inn's share of financial liabilities, one of those employers had turned out to be Gram Sweetwater.

Then he pictured his late wife, although he'd finally come to terms that he'd done all he could to extend her life. And when there'd been nothing more, he'd ensured she was kept as comfortable as possible.

He couldn't forget his recent failures. *Emerson and his daughter.*

While it probably didn't make a lick of sense to anyone else for him to resign, he saw it as a way to assume responsibility—and to make retribution—for his failings.

But at the moment, he faced a bigger dilemma.

Because now that Councilman Pershing had prohibited him from stepping foot on the grounds of the preserve, he felt he had no choice.

Raising his head to the sky, pellets of sleet stung his upturned face. He couldn't just sit around with Emerson potentially in harm's way.

And as his prayers ascended heavenward, soundless amid the flakes, he sensed the ever-present guilt and fear of failure fall away, only to be replaced by a different kind of fear.

The fear of losing Emerson. *Forever.*

Chapter Twelve

"Why does this keep happening?" When she returned home from a quick midday errand, Emerson's discovery of the trashed aviary had shot an arrow of defeat into her marrow. At spotting the mud smeared into the wire mesh, and the feeders destroyed, she'd just stared at the birds that now soared loose around the preserve.

With her recent attack still fresh in her memory, and concerned the perpetrators could be lurking within the shadows, she'd returned to her apartment before punching in Jack's pager number.

His declaration that he would send someone else to file the report still rankled. So it seemed that not only was she absolved of surveillance duty, but she was also smack-dab in the middle of another mess. And not the figurative kind.

Which spooled the wheels in her brain.

What if she was the one being targeted? Did someone want her off the premises?

Because even though the defacement began shortly before her arrival, everyone seemed to be convinced it would cease once she took full-time residence. But except for the recent short reprieve, it had continued to escalate.

After ending her call with Jack, she dove into

busy work to stave off her bruised feelings, which only stirred up additional questions. Namely: who would be assigned to deal with the latest damage?

As she puttered around the apartment, a flash of pastel hues grabbed her attention—the remaining balls of yarn she'd selected for the blankets she was making for the Christmas boutique. Her thoughts wandered to the tree lighting where she'd stood close enough to Jack to absorb his warmth. And how the three of them—Dewey at their feet—had squeezed together to view the spectacular event. It had been an idyllic evening.

But even though she'd wanted more from his invitation to stay behind, she hadn't needed to be told twice that the constable had yet to deal with his past, so that he could heal in the present. With the possibility of love in the future. Which also meant understanding that it wasn't his responsibility to shoulder the weight of the entire town. And that there was a refuge for them both if they accepted it.

But His name wasn't Jack.

The peal of her phone shattered the silence, scattering her jumbled thoughts like dust motes. Could Jack be on his way, after all?

Except that it was Lacey's face that blinked on her screen before she pressed the device to her ear. The rushed words her friend spoke sounded a lot like Jack had quit his job.

"He did what?"

Utter disbelief at the information Lacey shared seared through her.

"Persh said Jack stormed into his office this afternoon and resigned."

Grappling to comprehend this news, the significance settled in, compassion overriding her unanswered questions. He must've been wracked with anguish and confusion to make such a rash decision.

That's it. No more sitting around and waiting for the other shoe to drop.

This was her home, and she'd suffered too much loss to back down without a fight.

But before she plowed ahead, she could use guidance on how to cope with her feelings for a very stubborn constable and his adorable sidekick. The two of them a package deal in every way.

Rather than remain onsite to speak with the reporting officer, Emerson snapped several quick photos as evidence and sent them in a text to the part-time maintenance crew. With the preserve still closed to the public, the cleanup could be tackled the following day, although returning the birds would no doubt take a bit longer.

Next, she latched a leash onto Dewey's collar. Cruising through another batch of flurries, she parked in the lot at the back of Sweetwater Community Church. Upon trekking into the reception area, they were greeted with a warm smile from Marie.

"Doc, what a pleasant surprise!"

Skirting her desk, the woman enveloped her in a friendly hug, which calmed Emerson's nerves until Dewey's bark interrupted the moment.

Marie chuckled and scratched him between his ears, rendering him smitten. "How may I help you, dear?"

Before she could respond, Jack's daughter barreled around the corner with wide eyes.

"Mith Em! Dewey!" Josie's recent sprain ancient history, she tossed both arms around Emerson's legs before Dewey planted a sloppy, wet kiss on the child's cheek.

Josie giggled, causing Emerson's heart to swell as she hauled the child against her. "Fancy meeting you here." She inhaled her baby-fresh scent.

"Mith Marie ith watching me while Daddy runth around." Josie patted the knit hat covering Emerson's ears, her statement uttered with the innocent matter-of-factness of a child.

"The constable is running errands." Marie attempted to mask a giggle. "And your daddy should be here soon, so let's pick up your toys."

"Okay!" Josie slipped from Emerson's arms and scampered to the library adjacent to the compact office area, Dewey trailing behind.

As she remembered her reason for being there, Emerson stuffed down a fission of tension slithering up her spine.

"Would the pastor be able to spare a few minutes?"

As the older woman reviewed the calendar, Emerson admired her smart apparel and shiny silver bob. From what she'd observed, Marie was a beloved matriarch in Sweetwater, well-respected among its townsfolk. No doubt including the town florist, too. She hid a grin as she recalled the couple at Thanksgiving dinner.

Looking up from her desk, Marie clapped her hands together. "Good news! Another appointment canceled, so Pastor Mark will be free shortly."

Emerson breathed a sigh of relief. Although her counseling sessions in the city had been beneficial, her therapist had recommended continued support once she'd settled into her new surroundings. And she still hoped to work through her feelings toward the constable.

"Wonderful, thank you." Situating herself on a chair in the waiting area, she crossed and uncrossed her legs. "So have you lived in Sweetwater long?"

Miss Marie set down the travel mug she'd been holding. "My whole life." Her warm, blue-green gaze appeared focused on the past. "Lacey's Gram and I grew up together."

"Oh! I bet you have quite the stories about Lacey and Persh…" She pulled off her knit cap, fidgeting with the hem. "And Jack…"

Redirecting her gaze toward the library, where Josie tossed toys into a large wicker basket, her heart expanded with love for the child.

"Yes, indeed."

Emerson turned back in time to catch the knowing smile on the other woman's face.

"Gram and Pops both invested countless prayers on the behalf of all three." Marie clasped her hands atop her desk.

"I think they'd be pleased with how things worked out for good between Lacey and Persh."

"With a little help from the town legend, right?"

A sly grin curled Marie's lips. "I see how he looks at you."

"What, who?" Her fingers flew to her collar, loosening the scarf she'd retrieved from the back of her armoire.

"You and Jack are perfect for each other." The older woman straightened her back.

Rendered speechless, Emerson could only stare.

"I'm sure Lacey filled you in some on his challenging childhood. And the reason he tends to be so…" She paused, as if searching for the right word.

"Stubborn?" Eyes round, Emerson slapped her lips shut.

Marie chuckled as she fidgeted with her mug.

Sneaking a quick peek to confirm Josie was still occupied, with Dewey basking in the child's attention, she returned her full attention to Emerson.

"I don't want to speak out of turn, but I hope you can find it in your heart to look past Jack's sometimes-surly exterior." Her gaze never wavered. "And to take a risk."

Although confused by Marie's comments, her assessment of Jack's behavior was spot-on. She'd learned from Lacey that his past involved a secret family—the inciting incident that had forced him into the role of "man of the house" at the age of eight. But there was still more she had yet to learn about him.

Another wave of compassion washed over her, convincing her that both she and the constable needed to open up with each other.

A kernel of an idea sowed itself in her mind, derailing her plan to speak with the pastor.

"I've got to run, Miss Marie. Goodbye, sweet Josie!"

She was a woman on a mission.

Before returning to the scene of the crime, she and Dewey first made a quick stop at the local market to restock the dwindling cleaning supplies.

Rather than wait for maintenance to arrive onsite the following day, she scrubbed, swept and repaired whatever she could. And while on her knees, she prayed for the courage to be candid with Jack.

To give voice to the sordid details—from her ill-fated marriage to Aaron, to the loss of her baby boy, and to her inability to carry a child.

She hoped that sharing her own heartache would spur him to follow suit. Because it was the only way they'd be able to start over on level footing. Whether as friends, or something more.

The whole while, she'd been mulling over her idea until it had sprouted into a viable clue with the potential to identify the mystery vandals.

She believed that neither she nor Jack or the councilman had been looking for answers in the right place. Instead, they'd been working off the original assumption that the vandalism was an outside job, rather than properly considering the possibility that their perpetrators had been under their noses from the beginning.

Although she had a niggling feeling Jack may suspect her connection in some way, she knew otherwise. Before she mentioned her hunch to anyone, however, she had to be certain she was on the right track—without creating an additional mess, or getting the preserve shut down for good.

Despite Persh's directive to keep away from the preserve, and his resignation as constable, Jack had been prepared to disregard the councilman's command.

But when a page came through from the church office, he'd had no choice but to delay his plans. Especially after Marie had agreed to watch Josie, while he took care of business.

At least the proceeds from the wedding band had

afforded him the means to hire the security officer to double as his interim replacement. With that detail covered, the preserve would remain in capable hands. Although in his opinion, the only hands he wanted involved in Emerson's life were his own.

But she deserved a man far more worthy than the likes of him. Someone she could trust with her life.

Jack had ended up purging his heart to Pastor Mark, before taking Josie out for her favorite burger and fries at a popular bistro in town. Now, with his vehicle idling in the restaurant parking lot, and Josie in her car seat quietly flipping through the pages of a picture book, he palmed the back of his neck.

Head hanging low, he'd truly believed that resigning from his position as constable had been the right choice, along with his decision to pawn the ring.

Then why did it feel like he'd been socked in the gut?

"Daddy? Why are you thad?"

Risking a peek at his daughter, he traced the faint worry lines etched in the tender skin on her forehead, which only added to his pain.

"I just wish I could help Miss Em." And to fix things with the woman he'd begun to fall for.

But according to Pastor Mark, he first needed to accept forgiveness. Then he would find healing.

Josie tapped him on the shoulder with her mittened hand. "Everything will be okay."

Shifting into gear, he pasted a smile on his face that didn't quite reach his eyes. Because the only way for everything to be okay was to heed the clergyman's advice.

And the sooner he followed through, the sooner he and his child could move forward.

Whether their lives would include a certain dark-haired, dark-eyed veterinarian was not in his control.

Once father and daughter completed their evening routine, Jack retired to his customary spot at the kitchen table by the picture window overlooking his backyard, the solar lights illuminating the popcorn-and-cranberry garland woven throughout the bushes.

As the stillness enveloped him, he pulled an envelope from his back pocket that Marie had stuck in his hand when he'd fetched Josie.

A piece of misdirected correspondence had turned up in the church mail, his name scrawled across the front in familiar handwriting. Even with an absent return address, the postmark stamped on the envelope told him the sender's identity.

As he slipped a letter opener under its flap, with his free hand he pressed a fist against his chest, heart thundering beneath his rib cage.

A single sheet of paper floated to the table. Stifling a cough, he unfolded the stationery. The official logo at the top of the page spelled out Toby Witt, PI, Pine Ridge, Arizona.

He'd been waiting what felt like a lifetime for his questions to be addressed. Yet now that they might be at his fingertips, was he prepared for the answers?

Emerson's exotic face flickered in his consciousness, followed by a sudden need to have her by his side as he reviewed Toby's findings. In all likelihood, he was holding the missing piece of his childhood. And it was only fair to them both that he faced his past.

He began to read from the beginning.

Jack, I've located a blood relative of yours.

A low buzz started in Jack's ears as the walls in the room closed in on him. He paused, second-guessing the wisdom of continuing. But then his eyes latched back on to the words in front of him.

Technically, she's your half-sister. Kate Wells Simons, daughter of Clint and Veronica Wells. We spoke on the phone and she corroborated her identity and the information you'd given me.
She credits you for saving her life.

What?
Consternation muddied any coherent thought. Squeezing his eyes closed, he swiped a hand

through his unruly curls. It didn't take long before he found himself transported to his childhood home. The night his father walked out.

He was supposed to be in his bed sound asleep. Grasping at the fragments of his memories, he tugged on a minuscule thread to unravel the chain of events that had defined his young life.

There'd been no shouting that night, or banging of doors, that had lured him from his snug bed. Instead, an insatiable thirst had compelled him to leave his room. As he'd padded in his stocking feet down the hallway from the front of their bungalow toward the rear-side kitchen, the sound of murmuring in the living area beckoned him.

On any given evening, the television usually blared with the news channel his dad favored, while his mom read on the sofa curled up with a cup of tea balanced on the armrest. But that night, the TV screen was dark. It had been the whispering that forced him to pause on his way to the kitchen. With his birthday around the corner, he'd speculated their discussion involved the new bike he'd been coveting.

Curiosity had compelled him to hide behind the massive antique hutch his mother kept lined with fancy dishes he'd never seen her bring out, not even on special occasions. He hadn't understood her reasoning, until one day she explained how fragile they were, and that they could break easily. Even as an eight-year-old, he'd decided he wouldn't be that silly to avoid the enjoyment of something nice just because it might break.

Ouch.

He smacked his forehead. That was exactly how he'd been acting around Emerson. She wasn't a piece of delicate porcelain, but he'd been treating her like the dishware his mother had displayed in her hutch, afraid she might get hurt.

He filed that realization away as he returned to his eight-year-old self who crouched in his hiding place.

"You need to be with your original family, Clint Wells." From her position on the threadbare sofa, his mother spoke with a calmness she'd always possessed, her hands folded across her lap and eyes dry. "They need you more than we do."

That declaration. He'd blocked it out all these years, instead casting the blame on his father for his desertion. Yet all along, it had been his mother's insistence that her husband leave.

But why?

Searching the blurred edges of his recollections for a solution that made sense, a Christmas tree appeared and he smelled its cloying artificial pine scent. The same tree he and his mom had assembled each year and draped with handfuls of tinsel and macaroni streamers, and topped with a crooked star made of aluminum foil.

"But, Grace." His father's voice rang clear in his

mind as he pleaded, blue eyes like his son's darting to the hallway that led to Jack's room.

"Exactly." His mother tracked his dad's gaze. "I have our son." Rising from the sofa, she hugged her husband, then hefted a prepacked suitcase from the floor at her feet before shoving it into his father's hands.

It wasn't until the next morning when he'd discovered his father was never coming back.

Rubbing his eyes, he returned to the present moment, the darkness beyond the picture window evidence that nighttime had descended during his trip down memory lane.

From what he'd learned by reading Toby's letter and recalling the truth from that fateful night, the story of Jack's childhood had been rewritten.

He blinked, then picked up reading where he left off.

That's when he saw the kicker: his half-sister only lived a couple of towns over.

Shoving away from the table, he crinkled the sheet of paper in his palm. It was one thing to learn Clint Wells had harbored a secret family. But another to find out he had a half sibling—a woman he'd never met, and who'd been raised by his father—within driving distance.

Would she be interested in meeting her brother? Did he want to meet her?

Smoothing the page across the tabletop now, he perused the rest of the letter, his mind racing.

According to Toby, his sister, Kate, believed that had Clint Wells remained behind with Jack and Grace, she and her mother would've ended up on the streets. And to her, that made Jack a hero.

He snorted. If only she knew how far from the truth she was.

But that got him thinking. Only the last time he did that, he'd quit his job and pawned the wedding band.

Jack groaned as the sunlight that streamed through the window landed on his closed lids. Pulling the covers over his face, he attempted to blot out the last of the dreams that had plagued his sleep. From images of his father walking out, to a little girl with white-blond pigtails, to Dr. Emerson Parker.

Always Emerson.

Releasing a sigh that rasped against his throat, his heart ached. He missed the woman.

It quickly became apparent that Josie had also gotten up from the wrong side of the bed, which he blamed on his attempts to shield his daughter from further loss. Instead, he'd ended up depriving her of Emerson's love.

What an idiot I've been! He scrubbed at the breakfast dishes with fervor, trying to blot out his stubbornness that seemed to always get in the way. As demonstrated by his continued missteps.

The ding from his cell phone interrupted the

silence, reminding him that Persh expected to revisit yesterday's conversation. The one in which
he'd resigned. It still irked him to wait for a sec-
ond-hand report from the security detail, who'd
assured him that the veterinarian was safe.

But the text message wasn't from the councilman. It was from Marie Michaels.

Please pick up boutique items from B&B.

Before he'd left the church office with his PI
buddy's letter burning a hole in his pocket, he'd
promised Miss Marie he'd assist with the boutique, definitely one way to keep him occupied
and out of trouble.

His shoulders sagged. What he could use was
rest, but he had an assignment. And with preschool closed for the holidays, he'd be able to
spend more quality time with Josie. It would be
strange not reporting to the job he'd held for the
past dozen-odd years.

Come the first of the year, however, he'd need
to find other employment to keep a roof over their
heads. Maybe Persh could use another handyman.

"Daddy, can we go thee Dewey?"

He'd just retrieved Josie from his vehicle and
set her on the inn's shoveled walkway. "Not today,
Jose. We need to bring the boutique items to the
church."

His daughter's little face scrunched up, a pout

turning down her bow-shaped lips as she clomped up the pavement and onto the covered wooden porch.

He wouldn't mind releasing some pent-up steam in a like manner. Chuckling under his breath, he met her at the front door as a patron exited. Tipping his hat in greeting, he then escorted Josie into the welcoming warmth of the bed and breakfast. Immediately, she tugged off her pom-pom-topped knit cap and mittens and tossed them to the plank flooring.

Standing on tiptoe, she reached for a cookie.

He tapped her on the shoulder. "Where are your manners, young lady?"

"May I have a cookie, Daddy? Pleathe?"

His heart squeezed, the child's resemblance to her mother more prominent each day. "Yes, you may."

Shuffling across the floor and into the dining area, he was met by tables piled high with the ladies' handiwork for the upcoming boutique—rows of the hand-stitched and crafted wares carefully arranged.

"Hello-o-o-o?" Lingering in front of a variegated-blue crocheted baby blanket, his fingers toyed with the impossible softness. He'd seen a similar blanket when he'd been inside Emerson's apartment.

His gaze traveled the length of the table, marveling at each throw stacked atop the other made with different-colored yarns and patterns. But all fashioned in the same stitch, or so it appeared to his untrained eyes.

"Breathtaking, aren't they?"

He jerked at the sudden arrival of Lacey, his fingers stilling as she approached with one hand pressed against her abdomen, the other holding a glass of the naturally sweetened ice water that had put the B and B on the map.

She thrust the beverage at him. "Here, drink up."

Since he'd been around Persh's wife long enough to know better than to argue with her, he took a large swig of the refreshing brew.

"Who made these?" He hitched a thumb toward the blankets, although he had a pretty good hunch.

"Emerson did." Lacey shifted her attention to Josie. "Hello, my favorite five-year-old."

"Hi, Mith Lathey."

She stooped to hug his daughter, leaving him to his musings. Unable to tear his eyes from the afghans, he envisioned the love Emerson had hand-woven into each one. They would no doubt garner a good price at the boutique.

Yet it was the untold story buried within each painstaking stitch that tugged at his heartstrings, along with the haze of shadows that often dimmed the light reflecting from her dark eyes. How could he expect her to bare her soul when he'd kept his own locked up tight?

He gave himself a mental shake. "Is this all you need me to take to the church office?"

"The brunt of it." Lacey cleared the remaining tables and finished packing the items into large moving boxes that lined one of the walls.

Swiping an errant fiery strand that had escaped a bun at the nape of her neck, she threw her arms wide to encompass the homemade treasures. "I think this will be the grandest Christmas Boutique of them all!"

The boutique was another big tourist attraction, which meant more people would be arriving in town. Would that also cause additional trouble?

While no longer his concern in an official capacity, the consequences of his resignation drummed up a fresh wave of remorse.

He really needed to stock up on antacids.

Because not only had he left Persh and the town council in a bind, but he also had to trust that the money he'd paid out to the hired help would suffice until budgets were reviewed. Or he'd be saying goodbye to the extra security patrol at the preserve.

"Are you heading right to the church?" Lacey asked as she filled the jar in the entryway with a fresh batch of gingersnap cookies.

"I thought I might stop by Town Square first." He nodded toward Josie, whose legs dangled off the love seat in the living area where a fire crackled in the hearth, and lowered his voice. "And take this little munchkin skating."

"Good plan." Lacey smiled as she waved at the two of them. Once the boxes had been piled in the bed of his pickup, he pointed his vehicle in the direction of the church.

But a couple of blocks later, he pulled over to the curb.

"Why are we here, Daddy?"

Josie's bright round eyes spotted the ice rink in the middle of Town Square encircling the gazebo, which had been turned into a makeshift warming house. Children and families had arrived in droves to enjoy the afternoon's milder temperatures. Even in the High Country, the Arizona sun was surprisingly strong.

His daughter's sparkling gaze met his in the rearview mirror.

"Surprise!"

After retrieving her skates from the floorboard, he held them up by the laces and Josie clapped her mittened hands together, a grin stretching from ear to ear.

If only it was that easy to sidetrack this former constable from the ache in his heart.

Chapter Thirteen

As she finished tying the laces of her figure skates in the gazebo-turned-warming-house, Emerson watched other townsfolk and visitors enter and depart from the small space, children of all ages laughing while adults conversed.

When her friend had mentioned that the ice rink in Town Square had just been erected, she'd jumped at the opportunity to enjoy the fresh mountain air and engage in exercise at the same time. A reprieve from the ongoing drama surrounding the preserve had definitely been in order. Especially after her private investigation into the shenanigans had resulted in another impasse.

"I'm so glad you made it!" Annie beamed, her long blond hair gathered into a messy bun on top of her head. The black frames she often wore in place of contacts dipped low on the bridge of her nose as she strapped on her blades.

"There!" Annie rose, her ankles a tad shaky. Steadying herself with arms outstretched, she took a few tentative steps.

"I still don't understand why you turned down Josh's invitation." Testing her unstable limbs on the wooden planking, Emerson's wobbly legs resembled a newborn colt finding its footing in the world.

"I told you, no men in uniform." The other woman's tone was resolute, a glimmer of anguish dimming the light in her eyes.

Another man in uniform darted into Emerson's thoughts. Even though she hadn't physically pushed Jack away, she'd admittedly maintained her distance by shielding her past from him.

But the ball was in his court. And from where she stood, it was his silence that confirmed he wasn't interested in playing the game. Which meant she'd continue to extend friendship and cheer from the sidelines whenever possible.

Sighing, she hobbled next to Annie toward the door that led to the rink. "Ready when you are!" She flashed a tentative grin at her friend, whose topknot bobbed with each step.

"Let's go!" Annie grabbed her gloved hand, then steered her across the ramp and onto the ice. It appeared to be an elaborate setup, with the wooden perimeter holding gallons of water that had hardened into a glassy surface. Similar to a lazy river, the rink circled the warming house before meandering through Town Square.

Since the tree-lighting event, dozens of additional decorations had been erected throughout the gathering place for both pedestrians and skaters to enjoy during the daytime. And at night, thousands of glittering lights continued to illuminate the property.

Once Annie let go of her hand, Emerson tested

her unsteady legs just as images of Josie flitted through her mind. How delightful it would've been to share this experience with the child and to see it through her eyes. Simply imagining the awe on the little girl's face stirred the familiar twinge in her heart.

"Hey, isn't that the constable?"

Annie tugged on her coat sleeve, pointing toward the warming house that was now several yards behind them. Sure enough, Jack was crouched down to assist his daughter, who wore a tiny pair of figure skates, her pink cheeks aglow.

"It looks like it." Tamping down the involuntary thrill at seeing the two of them, she feigned disinterest by pivoting on her skates.

"Let's go say hi!" Annie took off in the opposite direction.

"I think I found my skating feet, so catch up when you can." Emerson scuffled across the ice, mindful to keep close to the perimeter boarding. Although she was no stranger to activities such as hiking and running, she could already feel the telltale ache from new muscles being worked.

Soon she settled into an easy rhythm, but when she rounded the next corner a little short, she careened directly into another skater.

"Oh, my goodness! I'm so sorry!" She craned her neck to peer up at the largest man she'd ever seen.

The bearded stranger steadied her with hands the size of salad plates.

"No harm done…as you can see." Cheeks ruddy, the man guffawed. "I'm Hank Valentine of Hank and Gordie's garage. But everyone calls me Big Country."

Sticking out his bare hand, he swallowed her mitten within his grasp.

"Emerson Parker, the new vet at the preserve. You took care of my flat."

Hank dropped her hand and yanked on his long beard. "Oh! That's right. Say, Doc, could I ask a favor?"

Delighted for an opportunity to return the mechanic's courtesy, she nodded. "Of course!"

Hank tottered in place. "I'm out of my element on the ice. Would you be so kind to accompany me around the rink?"

A chuckle spilled from her lips. "I'm not doing so great myself. But I'm willing to try."

Without another word, Hank offered his elbow and the two of them pushed off.

"Why do people call you Big Country, anyway?" Emerson turned her face toward the sun, soaking in its rays as they continued at a slow but steady pace.

"Because I'm as big as a country!" Releasing another belly laugh, he winked.

An imposing man such as Hank would normally have intimidated her, but the mechanic exuded genuine kindness in his pale blue gaze, not unlike the man who inhabited her thoughts.

"Look who I found!" Annie's wide grin stretched across her rosy cheeks.

Emerson gasped, seconds away from plowing into her friend, with Jack and Josie flanking each side.

"Mith Em!" Josie propelled her body against her ankles, which sent her reeling backward, arms flailing.

But rather than regain her poor attempt at balance, her hind end plopped onto the hard ice.

"Emerson!"

"Doc Parker!"

Both men appeared on either side of her, where they kneeled on the cold surface.

Her pride surely suffered the worst hit, stinging more than the tumble in part due to her long coat cushioning the fall.

A prickling started in her neck and traveled the length to her face. Her instinct was to blame it on the added attention, but the more likely reason was her proximity to the constable. She swallowed, the memory of their single kiss nearly keeping her grounded.

"No harm done." She averted her gaze from Jack's scrutiny, but not before she catalogued the creases etched into the skin around his eyes.

"I'm thorry, Mith Em." Tears filled Josie's eyes.

And when a hole in the ice didn't appear suddenly to swallow her from the view of onlookers, she accepted the hand Jack extended.

A zing skittered along her arm as she pushed to her feet, then jerked her fingers from Jack's grip before facing Josie. "I'm perfectly fine. See?"

"Will you 'kate with me?"

The child's eager expression warred with Emerson's promise to call in Hank's favor. And by the masked look behind Jack's eyes, she questioned his approval. Thankfully, Hank interrupted the awkward moment.

"Good to see you, Constable."

The mechanic thrust his giant hand toward Jack, who appeared taken aback.

"You too, Big Country," he replied, his words clipped. "We'd best be on our way." He picked up Josie and hoisted her atop his shoulders, her skates dangling against his broad chest.

Which drew Emerson's attention to his jacket that hung open, revealing the absent badge. But it was the missing gold band that delivered the rush of blood pounding in her ears.

"But, Daddy!" The tears spilled out of Josie's eyes and ran down her cheeks.

The unease of the moment reminded Emerson of the countless times when she'd been unable to gauge Aaron's thoughts or anticipate his behavior. Yet this wasn't her ex-husband who held her gaze for a beat longer than necessary.

Annie cleared her throat and tweaked the little girl's pigtails visible below the hem of her hat.

"Hey, maybe you and your daddy can stop by the bakery real soon for a special treat."

"Thank you for the invitation, Miss Annie." After tipping the brim of his hat at the adults, Jack disappeared toward the warming house with his pouting daughter.

"I hope I didn't cause hard feelings." Concern radiated from Hank's eyes.

She didn't know what to think from Jack's indecipherable expression. But if she'd ever hoped that the former constable might one day change his mind about her, discovering her skating with the mechanic had likely taken care of that notion in a hurry.

Which just might be for the best.

Except that now, her curiosity was piqued. And all because of the missing wedding band.

She was also still surprised that he'd resigned from his job. Because from everything she'd learned about Jack Wells thus far, quitting was not in his nature. Especially when it came to his calling.

Yet she'd practically done the same thing after losing the baby. In fact, she'd begun to believe that she was unworthy, and incapable, to care for anyone. Man, or beast.

But then the answer to prayer came by way of an opening at the Sweetwater Preserve & Sanctuary. And when the committee had welcomed her to start work early, she'd refused to turn her back on the opportunity to help those without a voice to heal. While she nursed her own wounds.

She'd love nothing more to offer the same support to Jack and his precious daughter. But she could only do so with the Lord's blessing.

After the fire chief had turned up at the rink and whisked off a reluctant Annie, Emerson and Hank cruised the rink. Accompanied by piped-in music, they passed by scenic wintry displays at every bend—from life-size plastic blow-ups inspired by popular holiday movies to a humble Nativity scene and human statues that posed as characters from the classic *Nutcracker*.

And with the shortest day of the year closing in, soon the sun's descent signaled the power to surge and the strings of twinkling lights to illuminate the square. It was in that brief moment she imagined Jack and his daughter by her side.

"Here we are!"

Hank's voice shattered her dream as he assisted her up the ramp where she'd begun.

"Thank you for humoring me, Doc. I think I'm ready to try another couples skate!"

A grin transformed Hank's ruddy complexion and he reminded Emerson of an oversized teddy bear.

She flashed him a smile, mittened hands on her hips. "Sounds like you have someone special in mind."

But Hank's attention was fixed on a spot over

her shoulder. Pivoting, she zeroed in on Josie and her father—Jack's focus glued to the two of them.

"Who am I fooling, anyway?"

Returning his gaze to Emerson, Hank's shoulders slumped.

"What are you talking about?" She placed her palm on Hank's forearm.

"Look at me, I'm like a bull in a china shop."

She squeezed his arm, then dropped her hand. "No way. You were the one who kept me upright, except for Miss Josie's exuberance."

Hank's face pinkened. "Thanks, Doc, and I'll let you know how it goes with the mystery lady." Winking, he opened the door to the warming house and invited her to take the lead. "Any more issues with your car, it's on the house."

She smiled her thanks at the man and tallied one more reason Sweetwater felt like home. And unless she heard otherwise, her plans didn't include uprooting her life anytime soon.

Yet she had a feeling that decision may hinge on whether a certain constable wanted her to stay… for more than a special event.

During her drive back to the preserve, muscles tired but invigorated, her resolve to fight for the preserve and sanctuary—a healing refuge for both animals and humans—was strengthened.

After arriving at the main building, she retrieved a wiggling Dewey from her apartment to begin rounds by double-checking the entrances and exits, as well as the hidden cameras.

As she completed the onsite safety checks Jack had walked her through early on during their surveillance, she attempted to staunch similar thoughts that had distracted her prior to her attack in the gift shop. In particular, visions of the precocious child and her handsome, albeit stubborn father.

His obstinacy no doubt stemming from trying to single-handedly manage the town's welfare.

But hadn't she done the same thing by aiming to fix Aaron, a task outside of her abilities? And not only had she risked her own safety, but also that of her unborn child. Which had resulted in the guilt she'd hung onto.

When her pass through the preserve was almost complete, she stumbled upon Petey and faltered. Black eyes piercing, he began to strut his brightly hued plumage in a slow, hypnotic circle, the magnificent sapphire-blue tail feathers fanning into an impressive arc.

By contrast, Dewey's fluffy tail curved low as he growled and then nipped at the peacock, causing Petey to flap his wings wildly.

A wave of uneasiness swept through her and she shuddered.

"What's up, Petey?" Striving for a calm, modulated tone, she returned his stare.

Quills vibrating, the large bird continued

to glower at his adversaries. And as odd as it sounded, it looked like Petey might be trying to tell her something.

"Are you hurt, boy?" She conducted a swift visual exam of the stunning peafowl's body, but spotted nothing amiss. "Or are you just lonely?" *She could relate.*

"Hang in there, Petey." Sidestepping around the feathered rescue, she gently tugged on Dewey's leash.

Yet as soon as she grasped the knob that opened the door into her office space, a chill slithered down her spine. A heightened sense of apprehension pooled in her veins.

"I'm just being silly." Shaking her head, she glanced at the pooch by her side. "Right, Dewey?"

But the tufts in the retriever's golden coat stood on end, his ears slicked back.

She should call Jack. Or 911.

Only there might not be time. Without thinking it through, she turned the handle, then pushed the door open—the air sucked from her lungs as Dewey broke free and charged. Angry barks bounced off the walls and…that odor. The same scent she'd smelled in the gift shop before she'd lost consciousness.

Mouth open, she took in the scene that she and Dewey had interrupted.

In time, she no doubt would be better able to describe the crazy sight. But the most challenging task would involve answering the question: Were they looking at vandalism, or would law enforcement label it something else entirely?

There was one thing she could be certain of, however. *Her suspicions had been right.*

If he'd ever considered how Dewey felt when the dog had made a mistake, his tail tucked between his legs and head suspended, Jack could identify. Because that was an accurate description of how he'd felt when he and Josie had high-tailed it off the ice rink.

But then his daughter had removed her hand from his neck to point toward the far end of Town Square, where a couple of teenagers topped off their version of a powdery-white Frosty with a cast-off scarf, twigs and stones.

"Daddy, look, a thnowman!"

The picturesque scene had reminded him of another reason he and Willow had remained in Sweetwater after marrying. Neither could imagine raising a child anywhere but the historic town.

"Maybe we can make another one soon." A simple reminder to himself to focus on his promise to create special holiday memories for his child. It wasn't her fault he'd made a mess of things.

"Yay, okay, Daddy!" She'd clapped her hands, his heart somersaulting as he recalled first spying the dark-haired beauty right before Hank had entered the picture.

It should've been him skating next to Emerson.

Several minutes later, Jack parked his car against the curb, where the church steeple was visible and served as a sign or a beacon of hope. He turned in his seat.

"Daddy needs to talk to Pastor Mark real quick. You can visit with Miss Marie."

"Mith Marie ith fun, but Mith Em ith funner."

He stifled a chuckle over his five-year-old's lack of tact.

"Okay, and I promise we'll go to the preserve real soon so you can play with Dewey."

"Yay!" Josie pumped her little legs to keep up with him as he strode up the walkway with purpose.

Over the past week, he'd entertained serious thoughts about adopting the rescue. But with the unresolved situation at the preserve, he'd settled for knowing that Emerson had the dog's protection.

And even though he'd learned from Persh that Carley had given her statement, she'd denied any involvement pertaining to the vandalism.

But Carley had pilfered the petty cash, explaining that it had been to help cover her side business. Word had traveled countywide about her mission to rehome missing animals, a passion she'd started pursuing in her free time. But an outpouring of requests had put her in a financial bind. Especially when she'd stopped cashing her paychecks for fear the preserve might be shut down permanently due to lack of funds. Persh had said the college student broke down in tears, insisting she'd always planned to pay back every last cent she'd taken.

His heart went out to her, and both he and Persh agreed that no charges would be filed. As long as she fulfilled her promise to return the funds.

Would the vandalism then stop?

"Hi, Jack… Josie." Marie rounded her desk and gave them both a big squeeze.

"Hi, Mith Marie, we went 'kating!" Jumping up and down, the pom-pom on Josie's knit cap bounced lopsidedly.

"How wonderful!"

Glancing sideways at him, without preamble the older woman pointed at the pastor's closed door. "Knock and go in."

He figured his angst must be written across his forehead with indelible ink by now. Following her instructions, he accepted the free chair in front of Pastor Mark's desk.

Assessing him with kind eyes and a calmness that Jack envied, Pastor Mark folded his hands atop his paper-strewn desk.

"What can I do for you, Constable?"

"Beg your pardon, Pastor, but I resigned from my position." The words tasted bitter on his tongue.

"Oh! That's surprising to hear." Pastor Mark

removed his reading glasses. "So what can I help you with?"

His thoughts coalesced, teeming with images and snippets of conversation over the past several weeks. Emerson lying on the hospital bed. Josie's injury. Statements that he wasn't responsible to watch over his "flock" 24/7, or that he wasn't to blame for his late wife's illness. Ending with the letter that informed him of a half-sister who considered him her hero.

"I'm at a loss, sir." Resting his forearms across his legs, he bowed his head. "I've made a colossal mess, Pastor."

Pastor Mark nodded before rounding his desk to place a wizened hand on Jack's hunched shoulders. "When I first started my ministry, I also treated my duties with the utmost importance."

He leaned against the edge of his desk. "As I should have."

Raising his eyes, Jack met the pastor's discerning gaze, which seemed to turn inward.

"But I learned pretty quickly that a minister—on call all hours of the day and night—is a poor substitute for the Lord, Himself."

Is that what he'd been trying to do?

"And that my role was about willingness and availability, and to intercede when required."

His attention riveted on the pastor, Jack's heart kicked into gear.

"When we say 'yes' to our calling, my boy, all

we need do is obey." The older man returned to his chair. "And to love those He entrusts us with for as long as we can."

Jack swiped a hand over his face, hot tears prickling behind his eyes. "I feel like I've been trying to do the Lord's job all these years."

Pastor Mark smiled at Jack, the creases on his face a testimony to his life experience. "So then, what's the plan?"

"I need to quit trying to play God, but then do what you said before. Forgive myself so that He can heal my heart." Rising to his feet, he shook hands with Pastor Mark. "And I know just where I need to start."

A knowing look crossed his pastor's face. "I'll be praying."

As the weight from the past three years finally lifted, he felt as if he'd been given a new lease at life. Closing the door behind him, he approached the reception desk with quick steps and a smile on his face.

"Thanks, Miss Marie, but the two of us have to run now because I'm on a mission."

He faced Josie, who stood at a chair coloring on a piece of paper. "Come on, kiddo, we're stopping at Miss Annie's." He peeked at Marie. "And then your daddy is back on duty."

The woman's eyes sparkled as he leaned down to swoop Josie into his arms.

But as the two of them headed toward the bakery,

he realized he might be too late. Because he may very well be the last person Emerson wanted to see.

Yet the fresh wave of excitement that coursed through his veins made it impossible for him to sit still.

He was finally ready.

Ready to make peace with his past. Ready to receive healing. And ready to accept love. He only hoped Emerson had a place in her heart for a mule-headed constable and his daughter.

During a quick stop at Annie's, he splurged on a cup-to-go of gooey hot chocolate topped with marshmallows for Josie, then dropped her off at the inn. He vowed to Persh and Lacey that he'd report back later. Just as soon as he'd dealt with a specific piece of unfinished business that was long overdue.

But first he needed to squeeze in one additional detour. Once he arrived home, as he jogged up the sidewalk, he viewed the modest gingerbread cottage with different eyes.

It was the house he'd planned to raise his children in, but it had been transformed into a home when occupied with the love of family.

And even though he and his Josie were a family of two, it was Emerson who filled the hole in both his heart, and their home.

Making tracks, he opened his closet door, then donned his best pair of work-issue slacks and shirt before adding a bolero tie and his "dress" Stetson.

After pinning on the badge Persh had returned without fuss to its place of prominence, he left the house, then grabbed the portable strobe light still in his possession and stuck it on top of his truck.

Guilt and failure no longer nipped at his heels. Instead, his heart was flooded with peace. He couldn't be sure if pawning the wedding band had been the first step toward healing. Or if it had been Pastor Mark's gentle nudge to get out of the way.

An image of Hank Valentine popped into his mind and Jack figured he might just have to compete with the town's most lovable bear of a man. Except that he and Emerson shared something that only the two of them could understand because of their shared connection—a painful past that required both forgiveness and healing.

Buckling up, he steered toward his final stop of the evening.

To ask Emerson to take a risk. On him.

Strobe light flashing in rhythmic rotations, he managed to stay below the speed limit, keeping pace with the setting sun and its dazzling array of pinks and oranges and violets. With the shadows reminiscent of that first night, months ago, when he'd stumbled into the vandalism in progress.

Or so he'd thought.

Instead, he'd careened into the arms of Sweetwater's new vet.

Slowing his vehicle, he rolled across the packed

snow toward the preserve. He flipped off the strobe light and lowered his window a crack before an eeriness began to settle in.

Although it hadn't been long since he'd last set foot on the property, the sounds he detected were anything but typical. Not only that, but the mid-December air hung heavy, like the calm before a storm. Or the tranquility of a winter sky as it unfurled and time stood still.

"Something isn't right." Cutting the engine, he muttered a prayer for guidance and protection. But rather than the cacophony of birds, notably Petey, that customarily greeted him, trouble seemed to be waiting to happen.

But he refused to travel down the long-worn rabbit trail of ominous thoughts because that was behind him. He should tell that to the hairs that rose on the back of his neck.

Senses on high alert, he unlatched the car door. the familiar jackhammer resonant in the stillness.

As if by rote, he reached for his holster, then removed his sidearm and released the safety. Crouching low, he sidestepped toward the building.

A high-pitched scream pierced through the night. His blood curdled as he launched himself in the direction of the clinic.

Seconds turned into minutes before Jack crashed through the double doors, his gun drawn.

His head swung left and then right, his attention divided by the scene in front of him. Swiveling first to face a mocha-colored, wide-eyed gaze, and then shifting toward four very black, extremely large eyes.

Except that their focus wasn't on him, or on Emerson.

"It's about time you arrived, Constable." Giddy laughter bubbled freely from the woman in front of him as she spread her arms. "Meet your vandals!"

Holstering his gun, Jack volleyed between bewilderment and disbelief as he gawked at the pair of four-legged, wily miscreants that grazed on tufts of hay littering the floor.

His chest swelled with relief. And more love than he believed was possible.

As the implications began to sink in, he realized his reputation was on the line. In fact, it would be pretty near impossible to live down the apprehension of these particular wrongdoers as long as he served the good town of Sweetwater.

But that was okay, because that was his plan. *To serve and protect.*

Once he'd finally cleared the air with Dr. Emerson Parker.

Chapter Fourteen

"What in the world is going on?" Rotating in a three-sixty as he observed the scene, Jack's boots left scuff prints along the grimy floor.

From the moment Emerson had interrupted the outrageous foray, she'd been attempting to lure the errant rescues back into their pens. But the culprits still blissfully grazed on the goodies she'd hauled in from the nearby tack shed. Time had been on her side, allowing her to process the situation. She chuckled at the consternation splashed across Jack's face.

But as relieved as she was to finally catch their vandals in the act, that didn't answer the question foremost on her mind. *Why is Jack here?*

Not to mention that something was different, his posture less guarded. And while the gold band was no longer pinned to his collar, the badge had been returned to its place.

She grimaced at the grazing miscreants. Another pressing question: How had they managed to escape from their pens and break into the clinic?

"I know about as much as you do." She brushed a strand of hair out of her eyes with the back of her hand. "But I sure feel better now that the alpaca and the llama are in custody."

A snicker erupted, her pulse tripping with anticipation. Was it too much to think Jack's arrival meant he'd undergone a change of heart?

Then Louie, likely sensing a threat, emitted a high-pitched alarm—a disturbing, almost human-sounding noise like the one that had preceded Jack's surprise entrance. Wincing at the shrill noise, she ran her fingers over his coarse hair to calm him.

"I don't understand." He pushed up his Stetson to scratch his forehead. "These…" He pointed at the pair of wooly mammals. "Are the vandals?"

"Well, why not check out the camera feed?" She retrieved a bucket and rag from the supply closet, and started scrubbing the debris that Louie and Alvin had dragged in from the grounds.

While she had hoped to discover the identity of the vandals by setting traps, she'd inadvertently led the troublemakers directly to the clinic. Thanks to her forgetfulness by leaving out her salad leftovers packed with apples, watermelon, carrots and romaine.

Although still in a state of shock, Jack slipped off his jacket and tossed it across one of the waiting-room chairs. "I'll see if Persh can pull it up. Let me help with the cleanup."

"You don't have to." *But did she want him to?*

"I know."

His intense gaze penetrated the last of her defenses as he stepped so close that if she were to lift her head, their lips would meet.

"But I want to."

Her chest rose and fell as his musky scent curled around her. Suddenly tongue-tied, she leaned away from him to snatch a couple of leashes. "Let's get these two back into their pens first."

The weight of his assessing gaze tracked her moves as she secured both animals. Pushing open the door, a blast of chilly air rushed in and she hunched her shoulders against the cold.

Working together, they led Louie and Alvin to the petting area, where Emerson stopped abruptly.

"What's the matter?" Jack's breath came in ragged puffs.

A fragment nagged at the periphery of her memory, but she couldn't put her finger on it. "Wait a second." Ensuring that the llama and alpaca were safely ensconced in their pens, she groped for an explanation.

Jack stomped his boots on the ground, slush spitting in all directions as thick snowflakes drifted from the sky, sparkling against the ground lighting.

As her fingers began to stiffen from the cold, she grasped at a conversation on the fringe of her consciousness. "The maintenance crew...some latch Josie mentioned." She was murmuring now, squeezing her eyes tight in an attempt to focus.

What was it Josie had said about a click?

Her eyes snapped open and affixed on the sign plastered to the gate they stood in front of.

Wait for the click.

Right there in big, bold letters.

"Let's get back, Doc. You're starting to shiver."

Just as his palm landed on the small of her back, she held up a hand—a slight tremor corroborating the constable's declaration.

"Hold on... I think I know what happened. But video coverage would help to confirm my theory."

"I'll text Persh." He pointed toward the clinic. "As soon as we get you back."

While Jack spoke with the councilman, Emerson consulted the visitor log, then reviewed her copious notes pertaining to each incident that occurred from the night she'd arrived at the preserve.

And there it was in black and white.

With everyone's initial assumption focused on the vandalism being an outside job, she'd begun to suspect just the opposite. But even then, if she was correct, she never would've guessed how it had all originated. What they needed now was corroborating proof. Yet even without it, her hunch was still directed at a pint-size, blond-haired sprite with the brightest blue eyes. A child who'd burrowed her way into her heart alongside her father.

But was Jack now ready to put the past behind him to forge a future...as a family? And to accept his innocence for circumstances beyond his control?

She, herself, had finally acknowledged her lack of culpability for the loss of her baby. Although she'd remained married to her ex-husband longer than she should have, she no longer believed she was to blame for his behavior. Nor did her inability to carry children affect her worth as a mother. Rather, it had been an ill-fated result of the emergency surgery necessary to save her life.

And if Jack was willing, she faced an opportunity to serve as a mother to Josie. Not in any way to replace Willow, but to shower the child with the love she deserved.

Gratitude swept through Emerson for the ability to find refuge and healing in Sweetwater, while at the same time starting over. Jack stood in front of her now with a look of expectancy on his handsome face.

Dewey snuffled to where she crouched by the bucket and nudged her side for pets. Nuzzling his neck, she averted her gaze.

If Jack and Josie were no longer part of her life, would she remain in Sweetwater?

While the answer depended on the future of the preserve, it also hinged on the man beside her.

Jack cleared his throat. "He's sure taken with you."

Peeking through her fringe of lashes, she watched him twist the brim of his Stetson between his palms, his strawberry-blond hair mussed. Her fingers twitched with the urge to smooth his curls.

Swallowing again, she fought to gather her wits, Dewey's coarse fur comforting as Jack kneeled on the floorboards next to her.

Scratching the dog between the ears, he traced her face with eyes that shone like azure waters, Petey's sapphire feathers and a cloudless summer day rolled into one.

"I—I still think that you and Josie would give him a good home."

"I was thinking the same thing."

His voice was deep, his gaze holding hers until she could barely hear over the erratic pulse pounding in her ears.

A phone buzzed, disrupting the charged moment. With reluctance, Jack peered at his mobile screen before holding up a finger.

"Persh."

Rising, he stepped a few feet away. Soon, she would learn if the videotape confirmed her theory.

Once she wrung out the dirty rag in the bucket, she instructed Dewey to sit before she tackled another set of muddy prints.

A few short minutes passed before Jack returned, eyebrows hiked up.

"Persh rewound the video coverage and saw something pretty…well, interesting."

"Let me guess." After draping the rag over the edge of the pail, she wiped her hands on her slacks and straightened. "Miss Josie didn't wait for the gate's click."

Bewilderment clouded his bright eyes as he nodded absently. "Once Persh noticed it in tonight's footage, he pulled a couple of recent tapes." He squeezed the back of his neck. "It appears my daughter is the common denominator preceding each visit by our 'vandals.'"

He added air quotes, emphasizing the absurdity of the situation.

Emerson rolled her eyes. If she'd strung the pieces together sooner, it would have saved time and anguish on everyone's behalf. Not to mention the added expenses.

But if there'd been any lingering doubts about her involvement behind the scenes, at least the proof exonerated her.

Still clueless about the reason for Jack's arrival, her eyes landed on his collar. Had he withdrawn his resignation and returned to patrol the grounds?

"You mentioned Dewey earlier?"

The shadows below his eyes conveyed his inner struggle. Something she had no control over. And if he wasn't in a position to do the hard work, then she would have to leave her job and the town behind. The haven of Sweetwater just wasn't big enough, and she would always want what Jack was unable to give.

In the wake of his silence, the catch in her heart confirmed what she'd assumed.

Pivoting away from his calculating observation, she blinked to keep the pooling tears from sliding down her cheeks. "I need to get this place in order."

"Can we talk first?"

She startled at the sound of his voice, her eyes snapping to his palms lifted in appeal and his Stetson back in place.

She'd made up her mind. *Hadn't she?*

Because with Jack's entire life devoted to serving and protecting those around him, how could he overlook her inability to protect her unborn child?

"Hey." Kneeling beside Emerson once more, with exaggerated gentleness Jack removed the rag from her hands then dropped it in the bucket.

His heart finally returning to normal, he reflected on the fear that had propelled him as he'd barreled into what he again believed to be a vandalism in progress. Fear that he'd failed to protect the woman who he'd grown to love with every breath of his core.

Which had caused him to stagger under the role on which he'd hinged his identity. Heart hammering against his rib cage in a staccato beat, it had vibrated down to his knocking knees, just as realization sluiced over him.

His identity had never been based on the badge he wore, but on the One who was his ultimate refuge.

And now, as he caught the mirth softening Emerson's exotic face, and the laughter in those dark pools of mystery, a lifetime of understanding coalesced in the seconds before the folly of the situation landed square between his eyes.

The irony was that his darling daughter had left the latch open to random pens located in the petting zoo, leaving Louie and Alvin to their own devices. While that did little to explain how they'd been able to enter the clinic or the gift shop, a more thorough review of surveillance records had also confirmed that the pair had been the mystery intruders when Emerson had been injured.

Regardless, he'd already made plans to replace each of the preserve's locks, even if that meant covering the expense with his salary. Which had been another aspect of his life that he'd made peace with during the past twenty-four hours.

It was not time to relinquish his badge.

He believed he still had a job to do, although he could use a financial windfall to garner more help at the station.

But if there was a will, there was a way—he could testify to that.

That old adage bolstered his courage as Emerson studied him with equal parts curiosity and resoluteness.

She recoiled as his fingers grazed hers, causing him to flinch. He forced back the longing to pull her into his embrace and kiss away the frown lines that marred her skin. Although he was finally ready to open up, he prayed he wasn't too late.

Coughing nervously, he reached out for Emerson's damp hands. "I've been a fool."

"Jack, you don't have to…"

Relief coursed through him as she allowed him to take hold, her fingers warming to his touch. "Please, let me finish."

Her doe eyes shimmered.

He gulped in a lungful of air. "I know I'm not to blame for Willow's illness and…and I'm ready to move forward." Exhaling the years of unfounded blame, his mettle soared.

"To love again." Memorizing every nuance, every shadow and plane on her face, his heart brimmed with promise. "And to make a home with you and Josie… and Dewey."

Emerson's brown eyes widened, her lips parting as if she grappled for the right words.

Had he misread the signs between them? For a split second, panic seized his chest. He had believed they could navigate together whatever past pain she held onto.

He trusted her, but now she had to trust him.

"I'm sorry."

Choking on a sob, she yanked her hands from his grip and straightened her legs so fast it sent him rocking back on his heels.

He had sensed they'd been on the verge of a breakthrough, but now as she disappeared from the clinic into the dusk, he feared what would happen next. Because he could no longer imagine a life without her.

Fueled by adrenaline and a race to make up for the time he'd lost, he nabbed his jacket from the chair, then dashed out the door. He located her immediately where the glow of security lights in the clearing revealed her whereabouts. With deliberate steps, he crunched through the hardened snow. Her attention fixed elsewhere, she appeared oblivious to his company until he placed his jacket across her quaking shoulders.

As if relinquishing her fight, her body melted against him.

"I owe you an explanation." Her voice was a near whisper amid the preserve's familiar cackles, cawing and snorts.

She leaned away from him then, and he dropped his hands to her waist to keep her from collapsing. He willed her to continue as his heart thundered in his ears. Surely she could feel it through her fingers.

"Aaron wasn't a nice person…but I stayed with him."

Her dark eyes begged him for understanding.

"Thought I could change him…heal him." She scoffed. "But that was never my job."

Her steady gaze held him captive and he didn't dare breathe.

"At the time I thought… I hoped…if only I

could be a better wife." She shook her head, a smirk tainting her full lips.

A tear tracked down her cheek, and he wrestled with his instinct to draw her closer. But she remained close enough that their hearts beat in sync.

"But when he struck me that last night..." She pressed a fist against her mouth, stifling another sob.

A stab of anguish tore into Jack's gut.

"I lost the baby I'd been carrying."

Those last words ripped his heart in two.

Forgive me, Lord. The rage he directed toward Aaron Parker burned like acid flooding his veins. He refused to lose it now. Not only would his wrath terrify her, it would do nothing to change the outcome of her tragedy.

Visions of the handcrafted blankets sifted through his mind, accompanied by a deeper understanding of the sorrow no doubt weaved into each one for a child she'd never hold.

And all this time, she'd carried the blame.

Picking up the subtle shift of her focus, as if embarrassed by her admission, Jack fully expected her to pull away. Which only compelled him to bridge the space, their breaths suspended between them.

"Neither one of us is to blame for what happened." His voice husky, it sounded more like a growl.

A shudder traveled the length of her and she hiccupped as her shoulders relaxed.

Ducking his head to peer at her from beneath the brim of his hat, he winked. "And now that Alvin and Louie are in custody…" He held his breath for the telltale sparkle in her eyes, biting back a tense chuckle when it appeared.

"I love you, Doc Parker." He swallowed then plowed ahead before he lost his last nerve. "And I hope you'll allow me to serve and protect you for as long as we're given."

Her arms snaked around his back and he smiled into her dark hair as he cradled her head against his shoulder. Inhaling her familiar lavender scent, it conjured pleasant memories from his childhood that he'd misplaced along the way. Afternoons in which he and his mother had pruned flower beds teeming with the aromatic flower—light and fresh with a touch of sweetness.

Despite the work ahead of them, his heart swelled with possibility.

For life after loss.

A sharp bark in the distance interrupted the moment, a reminder they still had the aftermath of Louie and Alvin's raid to deal with.

The woman in his arms half laughed, half sobbed into his collar.

"I love you too, Jack Wells. But are you sure you're equipped to take on not just me, but the entirety of miscreants in my care?"

Enveloped within the warmth of her embrace, he drew back mere inches and found himself nearly drowning in the depths of her mocha gaze that now shimmered with a different kind of tears.

Happy ones.

The woman clearly had no idea. Because not only did he plan to take on her and the entire preserve and sanctuary, but also the town council and backlash once the gossip-worthy fodder made its rounds.

And in the process of making peace with the past, he'd also come to believe the legend of Sweetwater was not just a one-time deal. Especially since there was definitely something in the sweet water that required faith—and a passel of prayers—to back it up.

"I wouldn't want it any other way."

Basking in Emerson's smile, and before either of them could come up with a good reason why they shouldn't seal the deal, Jack slanted his head to press his mouth against hers.

Everything faded in the background, then. From the bite in the air, to the snowflakes dancing mid-flight, to the cacophony in the aviary enclosure. And he barely noticed as the expanse overhead eclipsed into black velvet, while Emerson's hands trailed over his shoulders to wind around his neck, her fingers tickling the exposed hairs.

And as he held her within the circle of his arms,

much like a caterpillar safe within its cocoon, Jack felt he could've stayed like that forever.

But just as a butterfly whose time had come, the crumbling walls around his heart finally lay in rubble at his feet, a metamorphosis resulting from the greatest hardships of his life.

Dewey barked again, forcing them to separate with reluctance. Puffs of air hovered in front of their faces and their laughs echoed in the clearing. More than ever, he was convinced he could take on the world.

Although that wasn't his responsibility…and never had been.

He cataloged every inch of the flawless skin on Emerson's face and whispered a silent prayer. "How about a spring wedding?"

She tilted her head, as if to peer into the windows of his soul.

"Just as long as the alpaca and llama mind their manners…" She stood on tiptoe to press her lips against the rough stubble that lined his jaw. "It sounds perfect."

And then she planted a kiss on his mouth that pledged lazy family afternoons, evenings snuggling by a fire and creating a lifetime of promise.

It had taken a whole lot of heartache, but he'd finally gotten it right. Because instead of trying to rescue the veterinarian this time around, they'd ended up rescuing each other. With a whole lot of help from above.

Thanks to a pint-size, blond-haired, blue-eyed little girl and—last but not least—the legendary myth of small-town Sweetwater.

As he and Emerson returned to the clinic, their fingers laced together, he raised his eyes to stars too numerous to count. And he tried to imagine the competing display that would brighten Josie's face once she learned that, come springtime, Miss Em would become her mommy.

Chapter Fifteen

Christmas was just days away. Which meant only a few short months until she would become Mrs. Emerson Louise Wells, and mother to Josie Madelyn.

Yet none of the countless arrangements would've been possible to pull off without the assistance of her dear lady friends.

After the women had showered her, Jack, and Josie with well-wishes and blessings at the Christmas Boutique—where the three of them had shared news of their upcoming nuptials—her friends were quick to offer help with anything wedding related.

The plan included a simple affair at the Sweetwater Preserve & Sanctuary, where it had all begun, once the sun warmed the earth and melted the snow.

Refreshments would follow at the Sweetwater Bed & Breakfast, compliments of Lacey Pershing and Annie Greene. And oh, goodness, she still couldn't believe how the wedding had soon escalated to town-celebration status. But then again, she and Jack served as added proof that there was, indeed, something in the sweet water.

Privy to the truth behind the legend, a secret

smile tipped her lips. In fact, if any interested party visited long enough with the heiress and proprietress of the town's iconic inn, they'd learn the story behind the legend, too.

How the bed-and-breakfast—willed to Lacey by her grandparents, Gram and Pops—included a very specific addendum that read a lot like matchmaking. In layperson's terms, it equated to the power of suggestion, accompanied by gallons of water procured from a proprietary aquifer that created a sweet aftertaste, and was backed up by intercessory prayer.

Consequently, when couples began to hope for true love, it invited divine intervention.

Some naysayers argued it was nothing more than silliness. Yet the myth had remained intact since Lacey's great-great-great-grandfather Sweetwater met his bride upon the establishment of the town in 1864.

Emerson sighed, her chest squeezing with a tinge of sadness. She would've loved to have her dad and Aunt Francine walk her down the aisle, and to meet the woman who'd raised the man she was marrying.

"What about this store?" Annie stopped in front of a pawn shop on Main Street that sold antiques and an assortment of treasures.

"What's that saying?" Lacey opened the door, which set off the jangle of overhead bells.

"Someone's junk is someone else's treasure?" Emerson said.

Annie bumped elbows with her and snapped her fingers. "Exactly!"

"Do you have something borrowed and something blue?" Marie asked, her silver bob shining in the winter sunlight.

"Oh, let me think." Trailing behind the trio, she mentally assessed her checklist.

"You have the dress I wore on my wedding day."

"Yes!" As soon as she'd set eyes on the simple lace-and-ivory gown Lacey had volunteered, large tears had formed. How honored she was to wear her best friend's dress to stand before her husband-to-be and the councilman's closest ally.

"What about the blue?" Annie scanned the shelves and bins overflowing with various trinkets.

"I'll have to keep looking." Drawn to the antique jewelry displayed in a frosted glass case near the front of the store, Emerson peered at the treasures.

"Hi, Mr. Timmons, any new pieces come in?" Lacey joined her to peek at the merchandise.

"Hello, Mrs. Pershing and ladies."

The thick handlebar mustache made it appear that the shop owner wore a permanent smile, causing Emerson to stifle a giggle. He bent over to unlock the cabinet, then slid back the glass panel. Reaching in, he removed a gold band.

"Oh, something old!" Marie sidled up to the two women and peered over their shoulders.

As Mr. Timmons rose and lifted the ring with its brushed finish and delicate etchings from a nest of cotton, a hum filled her ears.

She was looking at Willow's wedding band that Jack had worn next to his badge.

Until his resignation as constable.

It all made sense to her now. How all of a sudden, extra security patrol had been hired to double his efforts. Not to mention the vacant spot on his collar.

And yet, the very ring that had tethered him to the past now waited among the dappled sundries and mementos to create new memories for someone else.

The delicate band propped on her palm, she played a mental tug-of-war. It had never been her desire for Jack to relinquish his happy memories from the past. But she couldn't ignore his decision to pawn the band. Especially if it had been integral to his healing journey.

Her greatest struggle pertained to what Lacey had shared about his original plans for the ring.

A soft touch on her shoulder interrupted the inner chaos, forcing her to meet the frown on Lacey's face.

"Hey...what's the matter?"

She blew out an exasperated sigh. "It's Willow's wedding band."

"Yes, Persh told me about it—that it had been missing from Jack's collar."

Lacey clasped her hand, her fingers enfolding around the small ring. "Something old," she whispered in Emerson's ear.

But how would Jack react? She refused to begin their marriage with added surprises. Yet the significance of what he'd done wasn't lost on her. His willingness to part with the one tangible memory from his previous life.

A vision of the blue blanket she'd begun to crochet after learning she carried a boy sparked an idea, then. How easy for her to fashion it into a shawl and her something blue.

That way, she and Jack would commence their new life as man and wife with fragments from their pasts. The happy pieces that—despite the hardships—had brought them to this place.

"Wrap it up, please." *And she knew exactly what she'd do with it.*

Handing her "something old" to Mr. Timmons, she beamed at the three women who surrounded her, a swell of gratitude threatening an ugly round of waterworks.

Everything would work out.

As long as a certain llama and alpaca stayed out of trouble.

But once the ladies exited the pawn shop, her

attention was snagged by Jack's long strides kicking up powdery puffs of snow on the near side of Town Square.

She hesitated as she caught the expression on his face, the telltale sign of worry etched into the creases around his mouth. Firm lips that kissed her with a tenderness that continued to be a healing balm to her soul.

Even after she'd shared the dark portions of her past with him, and that she'd be unable to bear children, he'd murmured words of compassion and understanding and promises that they'd entrust their future to God, their ultimate refuge.

Lacey was the first to speak up. "I wonder what's got the constable in such a tizzy?"

"Whatever it is, it doesn't look good." Annie's blond ponytail swished across her shoulders as she fell in line along the sidewalk.

An unseasonably warm winter day, the snow had melted off in most spots except for a dusting that had accumulated overnight. In fact, none of the ladies wore heavy coats. Except for Lacey, who'd been unable to hide her pregnancy any longer and kept her jacket unbuttoned.

Emerson stepped off the curb to meet her husband-to-be, who was bent at the waist to catch his breath. And rather than give in to her inclination of swooping in to heal his hurts, she instead strengthened their connection by sharing his anguish.

Except that the wedding band nestled in the bag she held seemed to have grown heavier.

Had she made the right choice? Or would the ring only cause Jack to backpedal through his painful memories?

"What is it?" Brushing away her concerns for the moment, she slipped into her professional persona as Jack straightened to his full height.

"Did Louie and Alvin escape again?" *Those sneaky miscreants.* She narrowed her eyes, recalling the latest discovery surrounding the two troublemakers. Even after extra care had been taken to click each latch, the animals had learned how to open several nobs and handles throughout the grounds.

Armed with that new knowledge, both she and Jack had invested their personal funds to upgrade the preserve's security. Although it had put a dent in their wedding reserve, thanks to the overwhelming generosity of the townsfolk and their wonderful friends, their special day would no doubt be one that legends were made of.

Jack jerked off his Stetson. "I wish!" Swiping back his curls, he shoved the hat back on his head where it sat off-kilter.

"What is it?" Lacey's eyebrows knit together. "Is Persh all right?" She rested a hand on her belly, wild copper hair framing her round face.

Only then did Jack appear to notice their audience along the curb. A flush peeked out from beneath his collar to work its way up his neck. "Persh is fine unless you count his vexation with the town council."

Her heart lurched, tamping down the impulse to jump to conclusions. "Tell me, Jack."

Taking her hand in his, her fiancé rubbed her palm with calloused fingers. "Bottom line—we've got twelve weeks to get the preserve up to code, and to raise enough for a new reserve..."

Worst-case scenarios spooled through her mind. "Or?"

Releasing her fingers, he opened his palms in resignation. "We lose the Sweetwater Preserve & Sanctuary."

"And my job." She couldn't believe this was happening since they'd come so far. Yes, she'd be making her home with Josie and Jack once they married. But she still had a calling, animals to care for. *Didn't she?*

"Sounds like it."

He rubbed his hands across her shoulders and squeezed, imparting as much comfort as possible with his touch, his woodsy scent enveloping her.

"Turns out the property's budget was cut in half under Spagnoletti's leadership, with the recent vandalism draining any surplus for the staff. Which means..."

"We need to call in the volunteers." Marie's hair bobbed in place as she spoke.

"Yup." Jack nodded.

Panic snapped at Emerson's heels. "With Christmas and our upcoming wedding…" Straightening her shoulders, she refused to start doubting the Lord's faithfulness. Even Carley's participation had worked out for good, because ultimately it had helped them to solve the mystery of Louie and Alvin's shenanigans.

"We've got this." She connected with Jack's bright blue gaze as it mirrored her spark of determination.

"That's why you're the brains of our operation." He winked, then pressed a kiss to her lips right there in the middle of Main Street. Downright oblivious to half of the wedding party's enthusiastic round of applause, accompanied by whoops and hollers that Emerson imagined could be heard all the way to the steps of Town Square.

Epilogue

❧

While he waited on the freshly trimmed lawn beneath the trellis interwoven with lavender and ivy, Jack surveyed the guests seated in the white folding chairs on loan from the church. He scanned the individuals who'd shown up to celebrate the occasion.

Parked at the podium was Pastor Mark, Bible in hand. His PI buddy who'd delivered the news about his half-sister gave him the side-eye. And then there were the Sweetwater Preserve & Sanctuary volunteers who'd escorted Louie and Alvin up the aisle to flank the wedding attendants.

He didn't try to stifle the broad grin that broke out across his face as the llama and alpaca, potentially groomed better than he was, strutted with long legs along the path where his daughter—Emerson's elected flower girl—would toss white rose petals, of which he'd plucked from their stems that very morning with painstaking precision and only a couple of mishaps.

He fiddled with the bandages on his fingers as a few snickers sprang from the crowd. At first, he'd been reluctant to include the two scoundrels in the wedding party. But it appeared his worries had been for nothing. His biggest fear now centered on the probability that his shirt buttons might burst, since he'd been unable to figure out how to express his gratitude—not only for their big day, but also for each day preceding it.

"Thank You" was far from adequate.

Because they'd succeeded. But it had taken a village—between their friends and community—to organize the wedding ceremony of the year within a few short months.

Not only that, but they'd also saved the preserve and sanctuary.

He shook his head, still amazed at the collective effort, including the largest bake sale he'd ever seen. As well as the sale of the cottage on Main Street.

He released a long sigh. Not one of resignation, but of acceptance, because of his confidence that Josie's mother would have extended her blessing.

It had all started by recruiting the assistance of Persh, Fire Chief Josh Rogers and Hank Valentine who, according to his wife-to-be, had a special interest in a new lady in town.

He snickered, picturing Lacey Sweetwater Pershing pouncing into the picture with gallons of sweet water.

And then, while Jack had bunked in an available room at the inn, the men built an addition onto Emerson's apartment to tide the three of them over once they married. In the meantime, construction of their new home was underway on a parcel of property near the preserve that he'd invested in many years earlier.

That would make it easy for his bride to continue her work with the animals onsite, and Josie would get to spend more time there, too.

Dewey barked next to him, the canine's smile and bow tie crooked, inciting the guests to break out in laughter. It was turning out to be a perfect day.

Once the cellist's fingers began to strum the prelude for the occasion, Jack snapped his attention toward the end of the pathway.

Swallowing his wad of nerves, he tugged at his bolero tie as his soon-to-be six-year-old daughter tripped up the makeshift aisle, a small woven basket dangling from her fingers and her hair tumbling in ringlets over her shoulders.

Yup, his buttons were near to bursting. Marveling at how grown-up she appeared, he admired the white, capped-sleeve dress, intricate lace, and beads hand sewn on by Gram's best friend and confidante. Josie's smile even revealed her permanent teeth starting to sprout.

Lacey Sweetwater Pershing appeared next in line, and he was pretty sure everyone in attendance noticed the glow on her face and the curved swell of her belly. Councilman Drew Pershing kept in step with his wife, their arms linked together, the couple still a perfect testament to Sweetwater's legend that true love prevails.

Even for a stubborn constable who reckoned he'd already had his opportunity.

Annie Greene and Josh Rogers trailed several feet behind. Despite the bakery owner's protestations that a man in uniform was off-limits, he sensed a softening beneath her resoluteness. Besides, Annie didn't have a prayer against Lacey's matchmaking skills, the endless supply of sweet water and the fire chief's persistence.

Marie and the town's florist, Charles, brought up the end of the wedding party. He pressed a hand to his mouth to cover another snicker, as he glanced at Lacey, but then turned his attention to the beautiful matching gowns the women wore, each sprinkled with a pale yellow-sunflower print. By contrast, the men were attired in dark gray suits accented with yellow bow ties, vests and single-stemmed dwarf sunflower boutonnieres.

After an interminable amount of time, in Jack's estimation, the cellist finally switched to playing the song he and Emerson had chosen for their special day—Johann Sebastian Bach's cantata Jesu, Joy Of Man's Desiring.

A hush fell over the gathering as the guests rose in anticipation. With Hank Valentine escorting Emerson—by way of the groom's blessing—Jack's eyes fixed on his bride as she proceeded up the aisle.

His throat working, he coughed into his fist. Although tempted to blame it on his tie, he had no doubt it was the stunning vision in ivory lace. With the "something blue" she wore draped over her shoulders a sign that she'd come a long way since her arrival in Sweetwater.

Dewey yelped again as he spotted Emerson approach the wedding party in short strides, her olive-toned complexion flushed in the spring breeze. An almost imperceptible smile reserved for Jack bowed her full lips.

As she faced him in front of the crowd, he took a deep breath and exhaled prayers that brimmed with thanks. And as he gazed at her, a literal button popped off his collar, his chest expanding with love, forgiveness and healing from above.

"Hi," she whispered in the shallow space between them, her exotic eyes searching his. *For doubts?*

He'd already examined his heart for the final time that morning, while he'd prepared for the big day. And the only thing that had turned up was gratefulness.

"'Hi' back." He wasn't able to conceal the foolish grin that consumed his face but he was beyond caring. He took a quick inventory of his attire, then. Dress uniform, complete with fancy Stetson. And his badge.

But now the wedding band he'd once worn pinned next to it hung from a dainty gold chain glimmering against Josie's neck. The "something old" that Emerson had asked to include in their ceremony. He snuck another peek at his daughter—who now stood alongside Dewey with as much seriousness as any five-year-old was capable. Treats had since replaced the white rose petals in her basket to distract the dog, whose fluffy tail brushed against his trousers. Chuckling, he cast a wink at his daughter.

He'd been flummoxed when Emerson had initially shown him the wedding band. Because not only had he pawned it to cover the security patrol, but also to put the past to rest. And to usher in a new beginning one day.

Yet he realized how much it had cost his future wife to purchase back the heirloom and his link to the past. Even then, that knowledge hadn't stopped her, so that he was able to present it to Josie, as he'd always hoped.

As a light breeze stirred Emerson's crown of rich brown curls, her lavender scent washed over him, and his focus returned to the woman who would soon become Mrs. Well. Thankful for her steady gaze, his nerves calmed as the cantata drew to a close.

As the guests returned to their seats, he grasped Emerson's fingers between his and applied gentle pressure in hopes of conveying a fraction of what he felt in his heart.

"We are gathered here today…" Pastor Mark

spoke the words that would commence their new journey. And then, in what seemed to be a few minutes, it was time to introduce Mr. and Mrs. Jackson Cooper Wells to all in attendance before they sealed it with a kiss.

But just as he dipped his head—more than ready to claim his bride—Louie and Alvin chose that moment to break free from their posts. Two pairs of gangly legs shot out from beneath them as they managed to entangle themselves between some of the sunflowers and ribbons tied to the chairs at the end of each row.

He should have known.

Because the low hum that Louie produced when all was right in his world—a little tidbit Josie had shared with him after one of her trips to the preserve—had all but disappeared during the ceremony.

And now, he could only stare, his jaw slack, as his spitfire of a new wife hitched up her long skirt to tear after one feisty llama and his unruly alpaca sidekick.

"You coming?" she hollered at him over her shoulder, wide smile and sparkling eyes brimming with unmistakable happiness.

"I'll head them off at Buzzy's den!" he shouted as he hoisted Josie onto his shoulders, then grabbed Dewey's leash.

And that's when it all came together.

With his family by his side, and God in the lead,

he was more than equipped to take on the town of Sweetwater…and yes, maybe even the world.

Or in this case, a llama and an alpaca. *No more and no less.*

* * * * *

Emerson's Whole Wheat Perfectly Sweet Cornbread recipe:

Ingredients:

¾ cup white flour
¾ cup whole-wheat flour
⅔ cup white sugar
½ cup cornmeal
1 tablespoon baking powder
½ teaspoon salt
1 ¼ cups milk
2 large eggs, lightly beaten
⅓ cup oil
3 tablespoons butter, melted

Directions:

Preheat oven to 350 F. Grease an 8-inch square baking pan. Combine flours, sugar, cornmeal, baking powder and salt in a medium bowl. Combine milk, eggs, oil and butter in a small bowl and mix well. Add to flour mixture and stir just until blended. Pour into baking pan. Bake for 35 minutes or until a wooden pick comes out clean. Cool for 5 minutes before removing from pans.

Dear Reader,

Thank you for joining me on my debut journey to Sweetwater, a fictional town based on a real-life "sanctuary" my husband and I fell in love with while vacationing in Northern Arizona's city of Prescott.

After I dreamt up the characters of Lacey and Persh, I realized the story belonged to grieving widower Constable Jack, his precocious daughter, Josie, and the wounded Doc Parker. While the book contains themes of loss and grief woven throughout many of our own life stories, my desire is that it delivers hope for new beginnings, humor—thanks to the miscreants behind the vandalism—and heart, for happy endings. And a reminder to trust God as our refuge and strength.

I'm planning to visit Sweetwater again, and I hope you'll come along for the ride. In the meantime, you can reach me through my website, chrismadayschmidt.com. And while you're there, be sure to sign up for my author newsletter to stay in touch.

Always,
Chris